I0525829

The Dragon Who Dabbled in Crypto
A Hardboiled Magic Adventure
TW Allen

Indignant Media

This story was brought to you in part through the sponsorship of:

- Laurie Ammaliatrice

- Ian Chung

- Jason Fliegel

- Vincent Jørgensen

- Mike Murphree

For more information on the Hardboiled Magic series, please visit:
https://www.magicdetective.com/

To subscribe to Todd Allen's newsletter (and get a free short story):
https://www.magicdetective.com/newsletter/

Books in the Hardboiled Magic series:

- *Student Loans Paid In Blood*

- *The Cursed Apps*

- The Dragon Who Dabbled in Crypto

Contents

Chapter One

The Digital Treasure Hoard

T he Hippie and The Swede sat down and turned on their respective microphones. It was time to record their podcast. No one was quite sure what their podcast was about, but that didn't seem to impede their popularity, such as it was.

"Should we continue where we left off last time?" asked The Swede.

"Before we do that," said The Hippie, "I want to talk about Schatzhorde des Drachen."

"Schatzhorde des Drachen?" The Swede was puzzled. "A German phrase? Doesn't that translate to the dragon's treasure horde?"

"It does," exclaimed The Hippie. "It's a new form of cryptocurrency. This one is unique because it's backed by gold."

"Isn't that the opposite of what cryptocurrency is supposed to do?" asked the Swede. "I thought cryptocurrency was supposed to be independent of physical commodities? Isn't that contrary to the point of cryptocurrency?"

"I like the security of it," replied The Hippie. "I want to be able to cash it in, for sweet, sweet gold. There's just one problem."

The hippie was interrupted by a strange tapping at the window. A tapping all the stranger for them being on the 10th floor. As they looked at the window, a tiny dot appeared and glowed red. The glass began to melt where the dot sat on it and a hole the size of a small coin emerged by the time the dot disappeared. Then a tiny red worm popped through the hole with surprising velocity. The worm flew through the air and landed on the table in front of them.

"What the hell is that?" asked The Hippie.

"It looks like a fireworm," said The Swede. "Hermodice carunculate. But that doesn't make any sense. Fireworms are aquatic creatures. They don't fly through the air."

"Since when did you become a marine biologist?" The Hippie raised an eyebrow.

"It's important to have hobbies," replied The Swede.

"Let's get this out of the studio," The Hippie stood up and reached for the worm.

"Don't touch it," cried The Swede. "The fireworm is poisonous. Those bristles around its edges contain a neurotoxin."

The Hippie pulled back, just in time for the fireworm to erupt into a ball of fire.

"Is that why they call it a fireworm?" asked The Hippie, stumbling towards the studio door.

"Not until today," replied The Swede.

The studio door burst open, striking The Hippie in the forehead. The Podcast Engineer dashed in with a fire extinguisher and applied it to the blaze.

The Swede picked up a pencil off the desk and used it to probe through the foam left behind by the extinguisher. What was left of the fireworm slid out of the pile and dropped to the floor.

"Is it?" inquired The Hippie.

"It's just as dead as we would have been, were we closer when it ignited," whispered The Swede.

Chapter Two
Sunk Costs

"How long has this been going on?" asked the man in the black suit.

"This is the first physical incident," replied The Head of HR, the other person in the room. "There were threats on social media. The Hippie was warned there would be consequences if Schatzhorde des Drachen was mentioned on the podcast. Naturally, The Hippie made a point of mentioning it and the attack happened immediately after the words were spoken. Like someone was monitoring them. Like it was premeditated."

"Monitoring them from 10 stories above the ground?" asked the man in the black suit.

"Does that meet your engagement requirements?" The Head of HR traded a question for a question. "An undersea dwelling animal melts through a window and bursts into flames? Unless we assume that it's just the ocean that keeps them from catching on fire under normal circumstances, would this be considered unusual? Is this a 'physics' problem?"

Mister Lewis had a business card that read "Physics Consultant," but that was something of an in-joke. Mister Lewis consulted on things that defied the laws of physics. Things that went bump in the night, lingered on after death and ate men's souls.

"It's out of the ordinary," Mister Lewis shook his head in agreement. "I'll be treating it as an assassination attempt until evidence establishes otherwise. Have they discussed supernatural matters on this podcast in the past? Or perhaps fishing?"

"Nobody ever knows what they're going to talk about. I mean, the show theoretically has a theme, but they seldom get around to it. They just sort of ramble on about themselves. That's their brand."

"Social media threats and a potentially taboo cryptocurrency," Mister Lewis frowned. "This is likely to require a little research. I'll probably also need to provide security for those two until we have a better handle on the threat vector."

"Their show has been drowning in red ink from the start," sighed The Head of HR. "What's one more expense in the name of diverse programming options? We will pay, of course. We can't have people taking shots at our employees."

"Who said it was people taking the shots?" Mister Lewis struggled to suppress a smirk.

"Very well," The Head of HR similarly failed to suppress an eye roll. "We'd provide protection for our talent that actually makes money for us, so we're obligated to extend the courtesy for all staff. And assassination attempts inside our building are a horrible look. Makes it hard to recruit. Please try to be swift, though. This whole thing is hemorrhaging money before it's even begun."

"I should probably start by interviewing The Hippie," offered Mister Lewis. "See if there are any known enemies, I should be aware of."

"You're in luck. They should be about to resume recording."

"Resume?" Mister Lewis abruptly stood up. "Does that mean they'll pick up where they left off? Talking about the same thing they were when they were attacked?"

Chapter Three

Cocky Conversation

"Whatever are you wearing?" asked The Swede.

The Swede and The Hippie had returned to the recording studio. The hole in the window was covered with a patch of duct tape and a folding table had replaced the one that had been set on fire, but the studio was more or less functional again.

"It's my new disco shirt," replied The Hippie.

"Listeners," began The Swede, "Our mutual friend here is wearing a shirt that's covered with... how should I describe it... large chunks of a mirror ball."

"Disco balls," corrected The Hippie. "Two entire large, Grade A disco balls were used to decorate this shirt. It's great."

"You were telling me about this treasure horde of the dragon," said The Swede, changing the subject as quickly as possible.

"Schatzhorde des Drachen," the words danced off The Hippie's tongue. "It's the way of the future. Gold-backed cryptocurrency."

"That still doesn't make any sense to me," said The Swede. "Why would you buy a digital coin representing gold, instead of just a gold coin?"

"No, no, no," interjected The Hippie. "It's not representing a cache of gold. The market value of the coin is backed by gold. Like when the dollar was on the gold standard."

"That's not what a gold standard is! A gold standard is when you base the value of your currency on the price of gold. A benchmark price. What you describe is the opposite of that. I understand that some people liken cryptocurrency to precious metals as a hedge against inflation, but how much gold would need to be accumulated to back it against the type of appreciation promised by cryptocurrency evangelists? They always call for 100x return, if not 1000x. Would not holding that much gold prove impractical, if not impossible? Where do they find it and where do they store it?"

"I've seen the pictures," cried The Hippie. "They have mountains of gold. Nobody knows where it came from, but they have gold."

"OK," sighed The Swede. "Let's just assume those pictures are real. I'll play along. What is the catch?"

"That's right," The Hippie leaped up as to better scream into the microphone. "There's a catch. It's on a private exchange and nobody's been able to cash it in."

"Are you saying it's not liquid?" asked The Swede.

"Liquid gold comes from distilleries in Islay," The Hippie was very nearly foaming at the mouth. "I'm talking about not being able to cash in my coins for solid gold. Oh, you can still buy Schatzhorde des Drachen coins, but the exchange no longer lets you cash out your assets. And everyone I know who's petitioned the exchange about selling their coins has disappeared."

"I see," said The Swede. "And how many of these valuable and desirable digital coins do you hold?"

The Hippie stared daggers at The Swede, which wasn't the most meaningful thing to be doing during a podcast.

"How did you know?"

"Tell the listeners how much you're in for."

"It's not that I'm in for that much," The Hippie's voice dipped down a half-octave closer to normal. "I got in early for not much... but it's a lot of money now."

"And what were you were planning on doing with all this gold you want to claim?"

"Quit working for the man," The Hippie's voice popped back up an octave. "If I could cash it in, I'd have enough to buy a small farm and live off the land. Grow potatoes and radishes."

"And mushrooms?"

"We will not talk about mushrooms," growled The Hippie. "But that's not the point. The point is somebody doesn't want anybody cashing out. It's a conspiracy. The Man is holding The People down and you know very well that the lizards are propping up The Man!"

Something thumped against the outside window and the conversation halted.

The Hippie and The Swede glanced at each other in nervous consternation and as their eyes locked, another thump came from the window.

"Is this going to be a regular thing?" The Swede said to no one in particular.

The doorknob on the studio door turned and the podcasting pair whipped their heads back towards that.

"Oh, Hell." When Mister Lewis opened the door, it wasn't The Hippie and The Swede who caught his attention. There was the shape outside the window. A shape like a serpent. With wings. And what looked like the outline of a rooster's head. "Hit the deck!"

Mister Lewis dove at the podcasters as the window exploded inward and glass shards flew everywhere.

"What was that?" The Hippie was under the table and attempting to peer out towards the broken window.

"Heads down," Mister Lewis grabbed The Hippie by the hair, pulling the head away from the direction of the window. "Eyes on the floor. There's a cockatrice flying around in here. If you meet its gaze, you're dead."

"Now see here," growled The Swede. "We do not discriminate against cocks on this program."

Mister Lewis bit his tongue, and the sound of flapping wings and hissing filled the conversation gap.

"That bird has a real gas problem," said The Hippie.

"Yeah, about that," replied Mister Lewis. "A cockatrice's breath is sometimes poisonous, just like their stare. Do you two think you could manage crawling over to the door? We should get out of here. Just keep your heads down and don't meet its gaze."

"What if it's landed on my back?" asked The Hippie.

In fact, the cockatrice had landed on The Hippie's back. It hissed and its breath came out in a tiny and mildly corrosive cloud that settled on the shard of disco ball in front of its beak. The cockatrice pecked twice at the marred glass before noticing the shards to either side of it. The cockatrice glanced left and noticed itself. It glanced right and, always having thought its right side was the handsomer side, gave itself a longing glance. The cockatrice's field of vision slid up and down its reflection before longingly gazing into its own eyes. Then its eyes melted.

"Is it safe to move now?" Asked The Hippie as the cockatrice's body fell to the floor.

"Don't look at," Mister Lewis began to yell before realizing the thing on the ground didn't have a head left and its neck was receding as it continued to bubble and liquify. "Never mind. Just don't touch the corpse. How did..."

Standing up and taking in the room, he realized what The Hippie's fashion statement was.

"Where do you get a shirt like that?" asked Mister Lewis. "Is it custom made?"

"There's a disco emporium up on Clayton," replied The Hippie. "They come in Small / Medium / Large."

"I might look into getting one," said Mister Lewis, leaning over the remains of the cockatrice. "Could come in useful in my line of work."

"Wait a minute," The Hippie gained a little composure upon getting a look at the cockatrice's corpse. "Is that a chicken lizard? Is it an agent of The Lizards? See, I told you The Lizards were keeping us down!"

"You can think of it that way if it helps, but it's not clear who or what sent it," Mister Lewis frowned as he reached into his inner jacket pocket and produced a pen. With the tip of the pen, he pried a small piece of paper off the talon of the cockatrice's rooster-like foot. The paper seemed to be clean, so he flipped it over and discovered it was a photo of The Hippie's face.

"Is this a publicity shot?" asked Mister Lewis.

"Give me that," The Swede snatched the photo. "No. No, I don't think I've seen this before."

"Why would somebody have..." The Hippie searched for the right words. "That looks like a wallet sized school photo of me. That's just weird."

"Indeed," said Mister Lewis, noticing the developing lab's mark on the back of the photo. "And that's no drugstore print. Somebody's spending money while they stalk you."

Chapter Four

Chasing the Tail

S ure enough, someone had spent a reasonable amount of money on a fancy photo lab to make prints of The Hippie's photo. It was an unusual size for a picture of an adult, so it was easily recalled by the manager. Perhaps someone thought an expensive lab would be discreet, but it wasn't a particularly large bill Mister Lewis had to slip to the manager to get the purchaser's contact information. It helped that the prints had been charged to an accounts receivable department. Mister Lewis was a little puzzled why someone would go to so much trail-leaving trouble instead of just using a laser printer, but he wasn't complaining.

The company that did the buying was the "Ophidia Trading Company," an import/export business that no one seemed to know much about, past that some basic business permits had been filed. The address was a warehouse, but at least a reasonably modern one.

Standing across the street from the warehouse, Mister Lewis peered at the building through a monocle, frowned, and then returned the monocle to his pocket. There was no outward appearance of magic to the building... but the assassination attempts had been conducted by creatures, not spells. It might not be a spellcaster he was looking for and the absence of magic didn't necessarily mean anything to his search.

Given the lack of information about the place and the lack of an aura around the building, Mister Lewis decided the best way to proceed was to rattle the cage... and hope nothing came out to bite him.

The front door wasn't locked, and the reception area was empty.

"Can I help you?" came a voice from the back.

"I was in need of some assistance with an importation issue," Mister Lewis called in the general direction of the voice.

"And what kind of issue would that be?" A shadowy figure emerged from a doorway at the back of the room.

"Sourcing exotic cuisine for my restaurant," Mister Lewis moved further into the room. "How experienced are you with animals?"

"Live animals?" The figure stuck to the shadows at the back of the room.

"Unless you can get fresh bushmeat delivered quickly enough to serve," Mister Lewis reached the center of the room. "And you are..."

"I am... the manager."

"Right," continued Mister Lewis. "So, I have a clientele with very peculiar tastes and I'm looking to source a new tasting menu. Securing the animals is not really the issue. Transporting them into the country is."

"Continue," said The Manager from the shadows.

"I'd like to start with a red bamboo snake for the appetizer. Probably cut up into nuggets. I'd probably need two or three of those. That would be followed by a bisque made of Inland Taipan snakes. I'd need at least

4 or 5. Then a filet of the Komodo dragon. Maybe two of those."

"Those are injurious animals," said The Manager. "That would be a violation of the Lacey Act."

"Well, you know... the laws of Man... but you do import exotic reptiles on occasion, don't you?"

"Who told you that?" hissed The Manager, leaning forward a bit and revealing a face covered with scaly patches of skin. Almost like a dermatitis or psoriasis outbreak, thought Mister Lewis, except instead of being red or silver, the scaly patches were more of a dull green.

"Oh, one hears things. Animal lovers have their circles."

"Animal eaters aren't quite the same thing as animal lovers. Your timing is good, though. I have just what you need in the back if you'll wait here."

The Manager stepped backwards through the doorway and was swallowed by the shadows. The sound of footsteps followed and then the sound of a desk drawer slamming. After two minutes, The Manager returned to the doorway, each newly gloved hand holding something. In the left hand, a rabbit, hanging by the ears. In the right hand, a knife.

"It's very important you know how to feed a Komodo dragon," The Manager spoke with the slightest hint of mirth. "Do you know what they eat?"

"In the wild?" Mister Lewis answered the question with a question. "Other animals, mostly."

"That's right," The Manager seemed to be suppressing a chuckle. "Meat. The dragon likes meat and adores the smell of blood."

With that, The Manager slashed the knife across the rabbit's belly, and tossed it to Mister Lewis, who caught it out of reflex.

"Very good," continued The Manager, dropping the knife to the floor and stripping off the gloves. "Now you're ready to make the friend you so humbly requested."

The Manager made an odd gesture as the right arm waved and a shuffling noise came from the shadows beyond the doorway.

Mister Lewis glanced down at his hands. The rabbit wasn't quite dead, but it was bleeding all over him.

A hiss came from the doorway. Mister Lewis looked up and saw six inches of a large, forked tongue flick through the darkness and into the light. Then it broke through. Running at him at what would have been a fast jog for a human was a lizard. A lizard that was around nine feet long and looked to weigh in the neighborhood of 280 pounds.

"Who in the hell keeps a Komodo dragon in a warehouse?" muttered Mister Lewis.

He threw the rabbit to the ground and started backing away. The rabbit tried to move but wasn't really up to it. That only lasted for a few seconds before the dragon ate it whole. Instead of belching and showing appreciation for a fine meal, the dragon turned its head to stare at Mister Lewis.

"What a lovely cologne you're wearing," cackled The Manager who snapped a finger.

A clang caused Mister Lewis to turn his head. An iron plate had fallen over the front door. A second clang and the window was covered, too. When he turned his head back to face front, the dragon was flicking that long tongue in his direction.

"They almost love the smell of blood as much as the taste," The Manager sniggered while stepping backwards into the shadows of the doorway.

Mister Lewis took two steps backwards, turned and ran. The dragon lunged forward and followed. It wasn't hard keeping ahead of the dragon. Komodo dragons were fast, as far as lizards go, but they couldn't run as fast as a human. Particularly a human with terror and adrenaline flowing through their veins. The problem was being in an enclosed room with one. That and all those pointy teeth.

The iron slab covering the door had dropped down from a railing above. It was too heavy to lift and there wasn't time to look for whatever button or lever raised it with the dragon charging. He couldn't retreat and on either side was a corner to be trapped in. Standing still was a worse idea, so he moved laterally to get a desk between himself and the giant lizard.

It was a moderately heavy and moderately old oak desk with a moderately new roller chair behind it. He picked up the chair and hurled it at the dragon. It bounced off, but that was to be expected. Komodo's had a thick hide that was effectively chainmail armor made out of bone.

The dragon paused before the desk, stood up on its hind legs, and once more flicked its long, yellow forked tongue into the air. Saliva, tinged red with blood from the rabbit, dripped from its mouth and the smell was not pleasant.

Mister Lewis winced at the odor and involuntarily took a half step back from the other side of the desk.

The dragon lumbered forward two steps, set its front claws on the desk, and snapped its jaw.

It was as much of an opening as he was likely to get, so Mister Lewis ducked down and launched himself into the desk's kneehole and threw his arms up as he pushed through, knocking over the dragon as the desk flipped on top of it.

Dropping it on its back really didn't hurt the dragon, but it bought him time to start running towards the back of the warehouse as the Komodo shrugged off the desk and found its footing. As he reached the shadowy doorway The Manager had disappeared into, the Komodo dragon was once more chasing him, swiftly shambling towards him in a motion resembling an alligator on angel dust.

He slammed the door and glanced around. It was a fairly standard warehouse. Crates. Dust. And an open overhead door on a loading dock at the far end of the room where The Manager presumably fled.

The door shuddered. It seemed the dragon had caught up. Unfortunately, a hungry Komodo following the scent of blood wasn't likely to get bored and wander off any time soon. Mister Lewis dragged a crate in front of the door. It wasn't much of a barricade, but it would have to do.

The door shuddered again, this time with the slight sound of wood starting to splinter.

"But those were precisely your orders," the strangely exasperated voice of The Manager screamed from somewhere beyond the warehouse.

This was followed by a sound like the wind blowing out a bonfire and a blast of heat that almost blistered Mister Lewis's skin, even though he had no line of sight with the source.

The door shuddered again, and the sound of cracking wood was more pronounced.

Mister Lewis slowly moved towards the loading dock.

Behind him, the top half of the door caved in and toppled over the crate and onto the floor.

Mister Lewis reached the loading dock and carefully peeked out. Nothing stirred outside. Then the sound of more crunching drew his attention back into the warehouse. The dragon had crawled through the opening that used to be the top half of the door, over the crate blocking the still-remaining lower half of the door and was once more charging towards him. He stepped outside the warehouse, reached up for the overhead door and slammed it down.

He jumped down from the dock and took a closer look at his surroundings. To his left, almost at the corner of the building, was a scorch mark along the ground in a shape resembling a human body. That stretch of pavement was still warm enough to grill a steak. Along the wall were flecks of ash and burn marks in a pattern that resembled blood spatter. It seemed likely The Manager wasn't going to be following orders any longer.

The sound of lizard hitting metal came from the dock. The Komodo was still hungry.

Chapter Five
Scope Creep

"B ut what happened to the Komodo dragon?" asked The Head of HR.

"I called animal control and let them worry about it," replied Mister Lewis. "It was the damnedest thing... the animal wasn't magical, but there also wasn't anywhere it could have been kept in that warehouse. I think it might have been teleported in from Komodo. It's probably a good thing I didn't inquire about a silverback gorilla. I don't think I could have outrun one of those."

Mister Lewis had returned to his client's office to report, but his findings were far from conclusive.

"So, you think this person," The Head of HR paused to search for the right words. "Conjured up those creatures that wrecked the studio and tried to kill The Hippie and The Swede?"

"There's circumstantial evidence. I just can't really tell you why. There wasn't a lot of meaningful paperwork in that building to tie management to anything. Based on the shouting I overheard, my best guess is it was either a contract hit, or someone was following orders from higher up the food chain."

"But this manager is dead?" asked The Head of HR.

"Vaporized," replied Mister Lewis. "The only thing left were ashes and a scorch mark. Someone... scratch that, something unleashed the equivalent of a blast furnace on that manager. I'm guessing that thing was either a client or some kind of upper management and it's highly unlikely that blast furnace was something that occurs in nature."

"So, this isn't over?"

"Doubtful. I'm not sure how much danger The Swede is in, but The Hippie absolutely needs to stay out of sight for the time being."

"How long is this going to take to clear up?" asked The Head of HR. "It would be helpful if you could give me a better idea of how to budget for this."

"I really don't know," replied Mister Lewis. "Whatever kind of operation that company was fronting, it was a very clean set up. It's going to take some digging just to know where to ask the next questions. And if that doesn't work... we might have to use your employees as bait to draw out whoever's responsible."

"I smell red ink pooling for that podcast," sighed The Head of HR. "Still... they're employees. We can't set a precedent of hanging them out to dry."

"What exactly is their podcast about, anyway?"

"I don't know," The Head of HR shrugged. "Nobody here's been able to figure it out. They have just enough of an audience for us to absorb their show. It's looking like a poor use of resources at the moment. I might be able to give you a lead, though I'm not sure how credible it is."

The Head of HR slid an inch thick manilla folder across the table.

"The Hippie has theories about a lot of things," continued the Head of HR. "It's not clear if they're based in reality, but it's good enough for that small audience. A lot of the broadcasts have centered around a wealthy individual."

"This individual have a name?"

"We don't say it out loud. It's also in The Hippie's contract not to say it out loud on the podcast. We refer to this individual as The Billionaire. The Billionaire is litigious and while lawsuits can be good for publicity, we don't need the added expense. Especially when the accusations are not sufficiently substantiated by documentation."

"I recognize the name," Mister Lewis flipped through the folder.

"It is thought that The Billionaire owns that export warehouse you visited. Not known, but thought. There are a lot of holding companies associated with The Billionaire and it's hard to prove anything."

"Oh, really?" said Mister Lewis. "So let me get this straight. The Hippie's been trying to air this Billionaire's dirty laundry on the podcast?"

"As blind items, but yes."

"And The Hippie thinks this Billionaire is... a lizard?" Mister Lewis stopped to re-read a page in the folder.

"Read on."

"And this Billionaire is thought to run the cryptocurrency exchange in question."

"That's not been confirmed."

"And this individual has a habit of shorting company stocks just before they implode... and then turning around buying the stock at the bottom of the trough before a recovery."

"That we have been able to partially confirm. At least that the shorts happened, and stocks were purchased near the bottom of the trough. However, it was holding companies executing the transactions. We have not been able to confirm the owners of the holding companies involved. Was The Billionaire involved? Possible, maybe even likely... but unclear from a strictly legal perspective."

"You spend a lot of time confirming conspiracy theories in your line of work?"

"When they're on one of our podcasts, legal likes to double check things."

Mister Lewis sighed, frowned and turned to the next page.

"And it is thought that your Billionaire is currently shorting a pharma stock?"

"There is a holding company currently shorting the stock," The Head of HR nodded in affirmation. "And, as it's written in the folder, the CEO of the company has been having a public meltdown."

"That's not really an unusual thing for a CEO to be doing in the current market," replied Mister Lewis.

"The stock being shorted preceded the CEO's erratic behavior by a few days. Did the short presage the behavior? That isn't nearly as clear."

"That's the hedge fund pattern, though, isn't it? Short the target, drop a damning report to the financial press and reap the rewards at the stock's price plummets."

"Except no report was issued. Just the short."

"Your Billionaire has some insider information on the CEO blowing a gasket?"

"Perhaps. But it seems unlikely someone could come across that kind of information before anyone else six times in the last year. And if they did, you'd think that would be impossible to keep quiet, so everyone would know about it."

"Hold on," Mister Lewis arched an eyebrow. "Are you saying this is the sixth time this has happened?"

"In each of the other five incidents we could confirm," The Head of HR continued, "the CEO of the targeted stock had a similarly volatile... incident that damaged the public perception of the company and its stock. Each time, the stock had been shorted a few days before the chaos struck. Is it The Billionaire orchestrating things behind the scenes? The Hippie thinks so, but as an institution, we could never have an opinion on that. At least not without documented proof."

"No, repeating rumors can lead to all kinds of trouble with a litigious subject. I suppose the question is ultimately whether this is coincidence, happenstance or enemy action."

"You would think there would be limits on how much coincidence one person could experience," The Head of HR nodded.

"Some experience higher levels of coincidence than others. But let's say I uncover some enemy action. Some of these theories point towards criminal conspiracies. If that turns out to be true, do you actually want that fully investigated and documented?"

"We could never officially have an opinion on anything like that or authorize something like that. We just need to make sure our employees are safe."

"I understand completely," Mister Lewis stood up. "Let me give these theories a field test and I'll get back to you."

Chapter Six
The Short That Dreams Are Made Of

T he press conference was not going well. The stock was in freefall and nothing The CEO did seemed to be helping. In fact, most of the trouble seemed to start with The CEO.

"The focus shouldn't be on me," The CEO attempted to yell, but it came as more of a yawn. It was a little too obvious the CEO was lacking sleep and suffering for it. "We have a wonderful product that's speeding its way through women."

"And which women would that be?" a reporter yelled above the laughter that erupted.

"Not women," The CEO's growl came off more as a whine. "We're on the verge of curing nightmares with the Holy Grail."

It was no wonder the cable news channels had begun covering these press conferences live. There was an entertainment value to them. The entertainment value of a slow-motion train wreck. Past that, the tried-and-true news philosophy of "if it bleeds, it leads" was in full effect. For the financial press, the bleeding was the company's stock. As the CEO's behavior and pronouncements became more erratic, the selloff had begun. Large bets were placed against the stock in the form of shorts and not even the social media meme-driven contrarian investors would come to its aid.

The ship was sinking.

"Alkaptonuria," screamed The CEO, coming back into focus. "We can cure alkaptonuria. There is hope."

"We'd like to hear more about the grail," a reporter cackled while mugging for the camera. "The women and the grail. Sounds like a specialty film."

"The women come at night," The CEO's eyes lost focus, peering somewhere beyond the horizon. "They dance around the lip of the Holy Grail, the cup that cures all ills."

"2 Girls, 1 Cup?" howled another reporter. "I've seen that one. Are you sure you aren't working on a cure for constipation?"

"No, no," The CEO stammered, lucidity making a tentative return. "Alkaptonuria starts with a darkening of the urine, not constipation. You're probably thinking of Hirschsprung disease. We have begun research on a non-surgical remedy for Hirschsprung, but we're nowhere near ready for clinical trials on that. It's still important work, though."

"What can you say to your investors about the price your stock is trading at?" another reporter shouted above the din.

"I cannot comment on the price dip," The CEO sensed a trap. "Circumstances have led to the market settling on a new price. Obviously, I disagree with it and potential investors should come up with their own opinions on what a fair price should be and whether we're undervalued."

"Is there a cure for being shorted?" yelled another reporter.

The CEO stared off into space, the unfocused eyes did not reflect contemplation.

"That's enough questions for today," the company's Public Relations Manager stepped in front of the podium to begin shooing the media away.

As the camera lights went off and the reporters returned their smart phones to their pockets, Mister Lewis worked his way around the edge of the room towards the podium. The CEO was still staring into infinity, so he parked himself in front of the back exit and waited.

Sure enough, after the passage of a few minutes, The CEO came wandering towards the door.

"I believe we have a few people in common," said Mister Lewis as he extended a business card.

The CEO absentmindedly took the business card. Focus returned and confusion appeared in The CEO's eyes while reading the card.

"You're familiar with the people at Cypticot?" Mister Lewis continued. "I helped them out with their... warehousing issues."

"That was you?" The CEO's perplexed look increased. "I'm not sure what that would have to do with me."

"You might be having trouble of a similar nature. I... am familiar with the way you've been staring. Here's the deal: I'm currently retained on a matter that may or may not be related to your stock market issues."

"You already have a client?"

"The matter might be related, but I'm not authorized to widen the scope. That doesn't preclude me from taking on an additional client, though. Call your contacts at Cypticot and tell them I thought I might have a line on your pain point. You'd be better off hearing it from them."

"How could you possibly know what my pain point is?"

"Because dreams can be haunted just like houses can," Mister Lewis smirked. "My number's on the card."

Chapter Seven

Dreams in the Pharma House

"Your references are excellent," said The Chief of Staff. "Disturbingly excellent. And I wouldn't have believed a word of what happened to them, if I hadn't known them for years. That said, I still don't understand how any of that applies to us or why you're here... but they made it pretty clear I should hear you out."

"It concerns your boss," replied Mister Lewis. "And in this case, it might get a little personal. I'm not sure I should be talking to an intermediary."

"The Board of Directors has made a decision to limit access to The CEO until... a few matters are cleared up."

"Begun negotiating the buyout, eh? That might be a little premature."

"Everyone involved would prefer an alternative," The Chief of Staff slumped a little in the chair. "Tell me what you can do. Tell me how this can be fixed. Convince me and we can walk through that door. The CEO's schedule is very open right now."

"The name SerpensFiscus mean anything to you?"

"Not as much as it could," growled The Chief of Staff. "They were the first one to short our stock, about a week before strange things started happening. There's a ridiculous chain of holding companies behind it and we can't figure out who the actual owners are."

"It's also Latin for 'serpent fund,' which might be significant," Mister Lewis leaned back in his chair. "That fund has popped up in... a matter I'm looking into for someone else."

"Something unusual?" The Chief of Staff raised an eyebrow. "The same kind of unusual you looked into for Cypticot?"

"Cypticot's circumstances were not premeditated," Mister Lewis frowned. "This may or may not be related, but I'm already poking around SerpensFiscus and what's going on with your boss might not be natural. As you may be aware, there seems to be a pattern at work."

"I'm aware. You know who's behind SerpensFiscus?"

"Nothing concrete enough to share, let alone hold up in court. Might be nothing. Might be something. But... as you put it, there seem to be a lot of unusual things happening in its wake."

"Are you saying our CEO has an... infestation?"

"You mean an infestation of the mind? If you want to put it that way, yes... it's a possible explanation. Or a corruption of the mind. And perhaps I'm wrong and it's just ordinary madness. Still, it would be better if you knew for sure, wouldn't it?"

Fingers drummed on the table. The Chief of Staff seemed on the verge of breaking out in a sweat.

"I suppose it can't make matters worse at this point," was the eventual answer.

The Chief of Staff stood up and approached the door of the inner office, produced a small ring of keys and unlocked the door.

"We'll lock this behind us," whispered The Chief of Staff. "We wouldn't want anyone wandering off."

The inner office was practically an apartment, swapping out an overly ornate desk for a bed. The CEO sat behind the desk, staring blankly at the wall with bloodshot eyes that didn't blink.

They stood in front of the desk for thirty seconds without acknowledgement before The Chief of Staff spoke.

"Somebody to see you, boss."

The CEO twitched, then blinked. The eyes became a little more focused, but not by much.

"This is the guy from yesterday," continued The Chief of Staff. "He might be able to explain some of what's going on."

The CEO's head shifted in what could have been either a nod or a muscle spasm.

"Bad night?" asked Mister Lewis.

"It comes and goes," said The Chief of Staff. "Today has been mostly like this, though."

"Tell me about the dream," Mister Lewis said to The CEO. "You had it again, didn't you?"

"Always the same," murmured The CEO. "It starts in the lab. The samples go in the centrifuge. The centrifuge spins. Then it starts to change."

"Change how?" Mister Lewis had started to walk around the room, inspecting the wall and tipping chairs to look underneath them. The CEO didn't notice.

"It spins and it grows. Grows into a cup. The Holy Grail, container of the elixir of life."

"That's not a horrible metaphor for pharma," Mister Lewis said to The Chief of Staff. "Is it part of your branding or something new?"

"Nothing we've used before," The Chief of Staff Shrugged.

"They drink from the Grail," shouted The CEO, apparently just aware enough of the people in the room to resent being interrupted. "They drink and are cured."

"Who drinks from the Grail?" asked Mister Lewis.

"The people," replied the CEO. "They appear and are cured. The elixir of the Grail cures all."

"And what about the women you mentioned? Do they drink from the Grail?"

"The women," The CEO paused to smile. "The women come after the masses. The cup grows again. Becomes a tower of healing. The women stand on the lip of the cup. They dance on the lip. Caress the lip. Then they fall in, and I join them."

"I get the picture," interjected Mister Lewis. "Do you only see those women in the dream, or do you see them in real life, too?"

"The dream is real," growled The CEO, jerking out of the chair.

"Of course, it is," said Mister Lewis. "But have you seen them outside the dream? Do they speak to you?"

"Of course," if nothing else, talking about the dream brought a semblance of focus to The CEO. "It's her job to talk to me."

"Whose job?" The Chief of Staff's voice rose an octave.

"Marketing," said The CEO. "My daily briefing."

"Oh," The Chief of Staff frowned and turned to Mister Lewis. "I forgot about that. She's new. Director of Marketing. Those briefings are just part of the job. I need to cancel that for today. We're following an isolation protocol."

"No," screamed The CEO. "I will see her!"

"Yeah," said Mister Lewis. "Maybe don't cancel that just yet. Just let me finish giving this place the once over before we get too far along."

Mister Lewis produced a monocle from his pocket, held it up to his eye and finished his tour of the office.

"I'm not seeing anything," he continued. "If there's a fetish or a totem in here, it's hidden pretty well and it's not active. If something is interfering with your boss's thought processes, it's not originating in here."

"You mean the infestation?" asked The Chief of Staff.

"I can't rule that out, either," replied Mister Lewis. "You've got an en suite bathroom attached to this office?"

"Of course," said The Chief of Staff.

"Then keep the meeting on the schedule. I want to observe it and rule out a possibility. And judging by the accelerated mental and physical deterioration, I'd better do it today. If somebody's started the final slide down the slope, this could be over quickly and it wouldn't leave much of a trail."

"Dancing," said The CEO, flashing a mindless grin. "A briefing and then dancing."

"Does the concern about your stock price pre-date all the strange behavior?" asked Mister Lewis.

"It's the subject of concern every time we have quarterly reports due," said The Chief of Staff. "The Street has expectations and there are consequences if expectations aren't met."

"Then that could be the way in," said Mister Lewis.

"The way into what?" asked The Chief of Staff.

"That sort of condition," Mister Lewis gestured towards The CEO. "It usually requires an opening to really get the claws into the mind. A worry. More likely an insecurity. If everything around here revolves around the stock price, it's something akin to a wound that can be picked at. Add a high profile shorting of the stock, that'll only increase the worry. Probably adds some second guessing and, if not, it would be easy enough to add some of that. Plenty of uncertainty to play with and sow seeds of anxiety."

Chapter Eight

The Loving Caress

"Are we ready for the brief?" The Director of Marketing stuck her head in the office and called out in sing-song voice.

The CEO nodded as a string of drool slowly drooped from the chin towards the surface of the desk.

"You've been doing such a good job," beamed The Director of Marketing, carefully shutting the door after entering.

The CEO nodded again. The drool had detached itself from the chin and lay puddled on the desk.

"So eager to please," said The Director of Marketing. "And we are pleased. In fact, I think we can wrap this venture up today. Are you ready for your reward?"

The CEO nodded a third time.

As The Director of Marketing approached the desk, her eyes shifted from hazel to a bright red that spread from the pupil to the iris and then overtook the sclera. As she rounded the desk, she raised her hands. While her fingers were long and thin to begin with, that wasn't going to suffice for what came next. The fingers extended until they all had a uniform length of eight inches. As they grew, the fingers writhed like snakes and the joints seemed to disappear as they stretched.

"Yes, it's time to end things," said The Director of Marketing.

Ten digits attached themselves to the CEO's head and the CEO's eyes rolled back, accompanied by a moan of pleasure.

The Director of Marketing's eyes began to glow and then throb. Her neck flopped backwards as though the spine had been removed and she made noises that sounded like a jungle cat purring, only wetter.

"Enough of that," Mister Lewis barked, emerging from the executive bathroom. "Snack time is over."

"And who might you be?" The Director of Marketing's head snapped back to an upright position and her eyes returned to hazel.

"Remove your hands from my client," growled Mister Lewis, stepping forward. "I'm not going to ask twice."

The Director of Marketing removed her hands and as she withdrew them, the fingers snapped back to a normal size.

"Nothing to see," she turned to face Mister Lewis with a smile and shifting hips. "I'm sure we can come to an understanding about this."

"You can start by explaining your relationship with SerpensFiscus," Mister Lewis hissed.

"I couldn't possibly comment on that," The Director of Marketing batted her eyes and waved jazz hands in front of herself.

Mister Lewis frowned and stared impassively at the display.

"Why don't we go over to the couch and discuss this?" The Director of Marketing said in a more tentative voice than before.

"Why don't you just answer the question?" replied Mister Lewis.

"We... we can do more interesting things than talk?" The Director of Marketing's eyes had turned red again, but all confidence had left her.

"What's the matter?" asked Mister Lewis. "Not finding a way in? Sorry if I'm not worried about stock prices or the effect of the weather forecast on Florida orange futures. I'm sure you'd have better luck finding self-esteem issues to exploit next door. I understand they're having a political rally. Then again, that assumes you're going to leave this room. That's a whole lot more likely to happen if you start answering questions. One more time: explain your relationship with SerpensFiscus."

"You'll understand if I choose to exercise client confidentiality."

"Oh, I'd understand it, but you don't have that option right now. You were a little slow removing the evidence." He gestured at The CEO.

"Then I fear we shall have to do this the hard way," The Director of Marketing changed as she spoke. Her legs merged together as though they were really a tail and the lower half of her torso coiled like a serpent preparing to strike. She raised her hands menacingly and hissed.

"Not buying it," said Mister Lewis with a sigh. "You can't claw me with those nail-less sausage fingers, and you can't get in my head. Save us both a lot of trouble and just give up your employer."

The Director of Marketing sprang and sailed across the room. As she landed, she raked a hand towards Mister Lewis's face and missed. Instead, he grabbed her wrist and swung, tossing her into the wall. She bounced off and slowly resumed an upright position.

"This isn't going to end well," said Mister Lewis. "Your kind are lovers, not fighters. I'm not real happy about you trying to finish off my client, either. You do not want to test me."

The Director of Marketing sprang again, this time with true aim, landing on Lewis and pushing him back a step. Lewis grabbed her throat, which stretched like a rubber band as he pushed her off.

"Beloved," screeched The Director of Marketing. "Come to my aid."

As the two wrestled, The CEO opened the desk drawer and started rummaging. A letter opener was produced.

Slowly, The CEO stood up and approached the fight.

Mister Lewis caught The Director of Marketing with a right cross. The Director of Marketing's head snapped back with the impact and then snapped forward again on the rebound, her mouth open wide as if to bite.

The CEO raised the letter opener overhead and brought it down hard. Unfortunately, the Director of Marketing's bobbing and bouncing head had gotten between the letter opener and Mister Lewis's throat. The point of the opener sunk into her head behind the ear. There was a squeaking noise as vapors escaped and a thin green liquid bubbled around the lip of the puncture. The Director of Marketing's eyes were open as she fell, her limbs suddenly having the rigidity of overcooked pasta.

The CEO stared at the uneven pile of meat on the floor and began to weep.

Mister Lewis rolled his eyes, placed a hand on The CEO's shoulder and said, "Are you with me?"

Chapter Nine

The Baiting Game

The Chief of Staff reentered the office to find The CEO crying on the couch and Mister Lewis dragging an enormous snake with the upper torso of The Director of Marketing into the bathroom.

"Boss?" The Chief of Staff tentatively approached The CEO.

"All my fault," sobbed The CEO.

"What happened here?" The Chief of Staff called towards the bathroom.

"Turns out you were right about it being an infestation," Mister Lewis stuck his head into the doorway. "You had a succubus in charge of marketing. Which, incidentally, sometimes works. They do tend to draw a crowd, you just don't one that's feeding on the staff."

"Succu... you mean a sex demon?" stammered The Chief of Staff.

"In a nutshell," replied Mister Lewis. "Although now we know why your boss always had sex on the brain. It was mandatory and enforced."

"Is she..."

"Yeah, she's a goner," Mister Lewis raised his voice as he ducked back into the bathroom. "Called your boss to her aid. Unfortunately for her, the entranced aren't known for their hand-eye coordination and she took the stabbing meant for me. The good news is, she doesn't seem to have any bones, so if you could get me something sharper than that damn letter opener and some cleaning supplies, I can make this go away. But maybe find a plunger, just in case."

The Chief of Staff glanced at The CEO, glanced at the pool of green liquid on the floor and followed a smeared streak of that green substance to the bathroom, where Mister Lewis was stuffing the remains of the Director of Marketing into a bathtub.

"Do we need to call the police?"

"If you think the media are a problem now," began Mister Lewis, "You wouldn't believe what would happen if something was found that was dead and not human. You wouldn't be able to offer a reasonable explanation for what the body is, and that would quickly lead the more... enthusiastic... reporters to engage in speculation about genetic experiments and scientific ethics. It's better for you if I handle this as quietly as possible."

"So, the boss isn't crazy?"

"No. Your boss is undoubtedly mad at the moment, but it's induced."

"Does that mean it's not permanent?"

"Too early to tell," Mister Lewis held up the letter opener, ran his finger down its side and then tossed it into the sink. "That thing's only good for puncturing. As for your boss, we now need to determine if your employee of the month was the only one feeding or there's more psychic mistresses floating around?"

The CEO was still in mourning as they approached the couch and didn't look up until Mister Lewis started tapping on the shoulder.

"We need to talk about those women dancing on the Grail," said Mister Lewis.

"She called and I failed her," wailed The CEO.

"I forgive you," said Mister Lewis. "But we need to talk about that Grail. How many women came to dance with you on the Grail?"

"She's dead. And it's my fault."

"You said 'women.' Plural. Were there more on the lip of the cup? Are they still alive?"

"You're right," The CEO looked up, not exactly hopefully, but perhaps a bit less devastated. "I'm not alone."

"How many more?"

"I danced with two."

"And do you see both of them outside of the dream? Or just your marketing brief?"

"They both come and play," The CEO's far away stare returned.

"And where do you see the other?"

"She's a face in the crowd. I can feel her in the crowd."

"Which crowd? Where is it?"

"When I walk around outside."

Mister Lewis glanced quizzically at The Chief of Staff, who responded with a shoulder shrug.

"Outside where?" asked Mister Lewis.

"Outside the building," a smile returned to The CEO's face. "She can always find me. It doesn't take long."

"Is someone staking out our office?" hissed The Chief of Staff.

Now it was Mister Lewis's turn to shrug his shoulders.

"So, you could take a walk right now?" asked Mister Lewis. "And the woman from the dream would come and find you?"

The CEO nodded enthusiastically and sprang up from the couch.

"An excellent idea," The CEO oozed happiness and headed towards the door.

Mister Lewis turned to The Chief of Staff, shrugged again, and followed.

Chapter Ten

2 Succubi, 1 Cup

It occurred to Mister Lewis that The CEO's focus seemed to revolve around elements from the ensorcelled dreams. On a mission to find the second dancer, The CEO's steps were even and the CEO's head was on a swivel... even if the eyes could have been less cloudy.

They circled the block once without incident. Instead of making a second circle, The CEO crossed the block and headed West, glancing around furtively for any signs of companionship.

Mister Lewis slowed down The Chief of Staff's pace, allowing a half block lead to The CEO. As they continued west, the crowd thickened up and three blocks later and it became clear what "she's a face in the crowd" meant. A face appeared in the crowd. A face you were not likely to forget and even the blind might notice.

The CEO froze.

An arm emerged from the crowd and beckoned, but The CEO stood firm. No matter. The face stepped forth from the crowd. There was a full body attached to it. She slid up to the CEO and wrapped her arms in an embrace. Whispering ensued.

"Be more clear," was the first whisper Mister Lewis could hear when he got close enough. "What letter did you open? Why aren't you in your meeting right now?"

"Don't treat it literally," Mister Lewis let the words slip out of a stone face and wagged a thumb towards The CEO. "Your co-worker asked for help from your thrall and caught a letter opener behind the ear that was intended for me. I had no idea those things worked on skulls, but it opened hers right up. You just can't find good mesmerized help these days."

The Succubus froze, shock in her eyes.

Mister Lewis grabbed her by the wrist and yanked her off The CEO, whose smile quickly faded.

"Do you always share a cup with a partner?" asked Mister Lewis. "In dreams, that is. I thought your kind didn't like sharing?"

"There are always exceptions," stammered The Succubus. "Some offers you can't refuse and there was enough treasure to go around."

"Yes," Mister Lewis narrowed his eyes. "Let's talk about that offer. Come clean and I'll keep the dazed wonder over there from sticking you with anything."

The CEO, noticeably distraught that the playdate had been interrupted, let loose with a loud, wet sob.

"You don't know what you're playing with," hissed The Succubus.

"That would be the point of asking, wouldn't it?" sighed Mister Lewis, tightening his grip.

"I will honor my contractual obligations," The Succubus declared.

Before he could reply, the arm of The Succubus changed. The wrist and hand dissolved into an appendage that most resembled a tentacle, and it grew slick as it changed. What had been her wrist slid out of his hand and The Succubus took off running, bounding away in steps that were a little too springy to be natural.

Mister Lewis tried to follow but wasn't as agile as The Succubus when it came to dodging people on a crowded sidewalk. The Succubus turned into an alley and by the time he got to the opening, she'd disappeared around a corner into a side alley that wrapped around the building. Two steps into the alley and he felt heat on his face as something flashed where The Succubus had fled.

He paused when he reached the corner. The edge of the building was warm to the touch. Carefully, he peeked around the corner and saw nothing. Cautiously, he stepped out. The side alley was empty, save for a scorch mark on the ground and the slightest scent of smoke.

Chapter Eleven
Cashflow

"P eople recover from this, right?" asked The Chief of Staff as they laid The CEO on the sofa.

The CEO was still overcome by the rejection and disappearance of the second Succubus. Coherence did not seem imminent.

"Sometimes," replied Mister Lewis. "Your boss is pretty far gone, though. Probably wouldn't have survived another feeding, but I don't think survival was intended either. If there were only two of them, their demise should have severed any lingering connections. Rest and time will determine what happens. Isolation and quiet is probably the best thing for now."

"You're sure this is over?"

"I've seen those scorch marks before," Mister Lewis nodded his head reassuringly. "Maybe don't let your boss be alone with anyone during recovery, though."

There was a knock on the office door. The door cracked open, and a head appeared in the gap.

"There's been some stock movement," said the head.

"And how is that important enough to interrupt this?" asked The Chief of Staff.

"You said you wanted to be updated immediately if SerpensFiscus changed its positioning," said the head.

"Pray continue," interjected Mister Lewis.

The Chief of Staff nodded in agreement.

"SerpensFiscus just closed out their short," continued the head in the doorway.

"It's over?" asked The Chief of Staff.

"There's more," said the head. "After they covered their short, they kept on buying. They probably poured all the profits on the short back into the stock. They're a major shareholder now."

"But why?" stammered The Chief of Staff.

"Because they got what they wanted," said Mister Lewis. "Either your CEO recovers, or you get a new one, then the stock goes back up. They profit on the stock's return to grace, just like they profited on the way down. It's slick."

"You know who did this?" fumed The Chief of Staff.

"I have suspicions. It's almost certainly related to that other matter I'm looking into."

"We want to be kept in the loop. And a piece of the payback when you resolve the situation."

"I remain open to additional clients," said Mister Lewis. "I'm sure we can come to an arrangement."

Chapter Twelve

What Makes It Money?

"Questions must be answered," The Hippie screamed into the microphone.

The Hippie and The Swede were recording another podcast. Their studio had been moved to the building's basement and it was more of an improvised vault than a studio. Acoustical tiles covered layered sheets of metal. The tiles also covered the protective runes that had been painted on the metal. The door, bolted onto the cage-like lining of the studio, had two titanium bars that slid across it to ensure it stayed shut. One at eye level and one at knee level. Nothing from the natural world was getting into that studio and neither was anything unnatural. Not even the sound of the lightning storm outside. A lightning storm that was confined to the block the studio's building occupied. Nature was not natural today.

"I have a question," said The Swede. "Why do you think this is a financial product?"

"Because it's a cryptocurrency?" replied The Hippie.

"Sure, Schatzhorde des Drachen calls itself a cryptocurrency," The Swede's smile was wide enough to be audible. "Can you actually spend it, though? Does anyone accept it for payment?"

"Well, no."

"Then it's not really any kind of a currency, is it?" The Swede ploughed on. "You have a digital item whose price is driven by demand, that you can't actually spend. If this item existed in the physical world, wouldn't we call it a collectible? For that matter, are you truly sure about its scarcity? Is there really a finite amount of coins or is that just what you're being told? Has anyone audited anything to confirm this? Anyone who's not associated with that coin?"

"It's a very valuable commodity," shouted The Hippie.

"Oh, it's a commodity now, is it?" interrupted The Swede.

"The only problem with it is the inability to re-exchange it for traditional currency," The Hippie was at a rolling boil. "And that problem will be fixed soon."

"Self-actualization is good. How do you propose to sell your coins on someone else's exchange, which it's not even clear you can access?"

"The identity of the Schatzhorde des Drachen owner is known to some of us."

"Don't say that name," cautioned The Swede. "You can't prove that's the owner."

"I know, I know," acknowledged The Hippie. "Our employer's lawyers won't let me say it, but some of us know. And one of us will be approaching... 'The Owner' before the week is out. There will be a reckoning."

"Now surely, you're not going to ambush this person? That could be dangerous."

"It's not me," said The Hippie. "But we know 'The Owner's' movements this week and someone trustworthy will be confronting 'The Owner' and won't leave until certain questions are answered."

Chapter Thirteen

The Name That Dare Not Be Spoken

T hunder rattled the windows in The Head of HR's office. The storm was getting worse.

"It's the damnedest thing," The Head of HR shut off the podcast and looked up from the computer. "The weather radar doesn't show this storm at all."

"Comes with the territory," replied Mister Lewis. "I suspect it will mysteriously dissipate as soon as The Hippie and The Swede finish their podcast. Probably an attempt to disrupt the building's electricity. Hard to record or broadcast without power."

"Oh, that happened with the first lightning strike. We have a backup generator. Time is money, after all. So, you're telling me you know who's behind it?"

"That you could prove in court?" Mister Lewis frowned. "No. But the shipping company tied to the initial assassination attempt and The Hippie's stock tip are almost certainly related. It's very unusual for beings to be reduced to scorch marks so quickly. It strains the definition of coincidence to encounter such a thing twice without the incidents being related. When we know what caused the scorch marks, we'll still have to see how it ties things together, but it will lead to a name."

"I didn't think this kind of a problem made it to court?" asked The Head of HR.

"Oh, there are sometimes civil suits for damages and lost earnings, depending on how things have manifested. That's not the norm, though. Still, it would be a bad idea to confront anyone and force their hand until we have a little better idea of what we're dealing with and how many entities are involved. Bodies turned to ash, followed up with this storm? That's not beginner stuff."

"Then what do you propose to do next?"

"I think it's time I laid eyes on…" Mister Lewis shifted in his chair. "How did you want to refer to this…"

"The Billionaire," interjected The Head of HR. "Legal has confirmed that term is generic enough to avoid liability."

"So be it. I don't suppose it's known where these billions come from by any chance?"

"That we know of? As you've already figured out, there seems to be a great deal of stock trading that may or may not be shady."

"I'm going with definitely shady on that," said Mister Lewis.

"Then you'll also love the gambling income. It's been observed our Billionaire will bet on just about anything. There's palladium mining in Guatemala that provides a sizeable income."

"That's a strange place for palladium mining."

"We're at the point, if something about this wasn't strange, I'd start to get worried," replied The Head of HR with an eye roll. "And then there are a smattering of smaller businesses. Import/export. Warehouses. Even a pawn shop. There are a lot of shell companies involved.

Some of this is rumor, but The Hippie's friends seem to be right about these things more often than not. They do seem motivated."

"Then I think it's time I laid eyes on this Billionaire of yours in person," Mister Lewis managed to keep his own eyes from rolling. Barely. "And if The Hippie has a friend raising a ruckus, it might be instructive to sit back and watch."

"Normally, we would advise our employees to avoid dangerous situations. Do you think there's the potential for violence?"

"The trail of ashes would make you think so, wouldn't it? The Hippie's friend is taking an awful risk by forcing a confrontation, but they probably don't understand what they're playing with. Then again, neither do I. That's why I need to be there. Watch the reaction. See if I can spot who or what The Billionaire is using as an enforcer or an incinerator. Understand what the trap really is. Hopefully, any confrontation is in public, where there's less likely to be violence. If a confrontation causes The Billionaire's hand to be tipped, I'm hoping I can get a look at what's creating those scorch marks... and maybe get the interloper out of there before there's a barbeque. Besides, we haven't established that The Billionaire is calling the shots yet. At the center of it, sure, but it's causality vs. correlation until we know more. Do your notes include The Billionaire's schedule for the week or is The Hippie not sharing that?"

"We have that," The Head of HR started tapping and swiping on a tablet. "The Billionaire will be at an eSports tournament this week. It's supposed to be some kind of gambling trip, but it's not clear if The Billionaire is personally gambling on the games or is starting up a sportsbook. There are rumors about playing on both sides of the ledger."

"This is a public event?"

"Ticketed, but tickets are available to the general public."

"Then I suppose I should familiarize myself with proposition bets at eSporting events. There's nothing worse than walking into a racetrack blind."

Chapter Fourteen

The Sporting Life

W hen Mister Lewis walked into the eSports arena, the tournament was already in full swing. In many ways it felt more like a convention center than a conventional sports arena. Instead of the sport being in the center of the building, surrounded by seats, the action took place in a large theater at the back of the building. The only thing in the place that resembled a stadium was a block of stadium style movie theater seating facing a stage that housed the competing teams of gamers. Above the stage hung an enormous LED screen flipping between the various scrimmages in the game and showing scores.

The game was a medieval affair with wizards and Vikings ambushing each other as they sought treasure in a dungeon. It wasn't clear why the Vikings were wielding katanas, but perhaps that's why they called it fantasy gaming?

Mister Lewis didn't see his quarry, so he withdrew to the outer rooms. The arena had a variety of suites designed to separate the attendees from their currency.

The first room was a video game room. Retro arcade cabinets stood in stark contrast to the modern mayhem being played out by the teams on stage. In the time-honored tradition of stadium pricing, a game of Tron would run five dollars with non-refundable tokens available from a change machine in the corner.

The second room was the bar. It would have to be, but the dynamic was a little different than the typical stadium bar. Since a good chunk of the lounge lizards were underage, this place was checking IDs much harder than the typical stadium bar and almost everyone was drinking plastic cups of fizzy liquids that didn't quite look like cocktails.

The third room had a bit more action. It was the betting room, and it was almost as fancy as the theater. The walls were lined with screens. The first column of gameplay from different player perspectives, the second column featuring odds on various wagers and the progress towards them. Flanking those columns were widescreens of the players on stage in the theater section.

In the middle of the room, sporting a wide grin with a few too many teeth, was The Billionaire.

Mister Lewis reached into his pocket for his monocle, as he strolled out of The Billionaire's line of sight. A quick glance through the monocle revealed nothing. No illusions, no active spells. What his eyes showed him was what was physically there.

Mister Lewis slipped the monocle back in his pocket and backed up to the bar room in search of a prop.

"Rye," he told The Bartender after scanning the beer taps and wincing. "Neat."

The Bartender stared back blankly.

"You don't have rye?" asked Mister Lewis.

"Thank god," shouted The Bartender.

Mister Lewis tilted his head and quizzically peered over his sunglasses.

"You ordered a drink," exclaimed The Bartender.

"That is the point of having a bar?"

"You ordered a real drink," The Bartender's hands shook while rummaging through the well for a bottle. "Look around you. They're all drinking Mountain Dew. Or Mountain Dew with a shot of Red Bull."

"Caffeine culture," replied Mister Lewis. "Comes with the territory."

The bartender slammed a rocks glass on the bar and poured a double in a jittery motion that could have been flair or could have been frayed nerves.

"On the house," The Bartender said a bit too loudly, while glaring at the rest of the room. "You drink, lest civilization collapse."

Mister Lewis threw a ten-dollar bill on the bar and slid back towards the betting parlor.

The Billionaire was at the betting window and seemed to be insisting on payment in cash.

"What's your system for these proposition bets?" The Ticket Writer asked in an only partially friendly tone.

"The Chest of Angry Blizzards," The Billionaire said with a malicious smile, counting out half the winnings and sliding them towards The Ticket Writer, while pocketing the remaining half. "Team Ptool will reach it first. All of this on them."

The Billionaire palmed the resulting betting slip and slunk off to watch the video screen.

Mister Lewis paused for a moment, appraised the betting line and slid up to the betting window.

"$20 on Team Ptool to be the first to the Chest of Angry Blizzards."

The Ticket Writer silently slid a receipt through the window.

"Is it unusual to have an in-person booth for eSports?" asked Mister Lewis.

"We have some... high volume customers who prefer the in-person experience to online betting," replied The Ticket Writer.

"And nice, untraceable cash winnings?"

"Some of our biggest winners prefer cash," The Ticket Writer said with a frown. "Hold on to that receipt and you'll likely be able to acquire some cash yourself. The last person to place a bet on Team Ptool very rarely loses."

"You say the owner doesn't lose?"

"Not very often," The Ticket Writer glanced back and forth between The Billionaire and Mister Lewis with narrowed eyes. "Not many people know about the owner. Who are you, exactly?"

"Oh, I just meant the house never loses," Mister Lewis offered.

"Riiiiiight," The Ticket Writer wasn't buying. "Hang on to the ticket anyway."

Chapter Fifteen
Stacked Decks Can Be Digital

The Billionaire stayed in the betting room, watching the screens. Specifically, watching the column of screens showing the in-game view. The betting slip was folded between The Billionaire's fingers and its edges were getting rubbed between the thumb, middle and index fingers in the universal gesture for money.

Mister Lewis slid to the back of the room, eyed his betting slip and wondered just exactly what this Chest of Angry Blizzards was? He figured the main difference between himself and the average better in the room was he knew full well that he had no idea what he was betting on. As long as no one figured that out, he ought to fit in, so long as he showed the right reaction to however the bet turned out.

On the in-game screens, squads of Vikings with Katanas traversed the game's landscape, slicing their way through monsters and threatening to converge on an icon that could have possibly been a chest if the game producers had spent a little more money on art and design. He figured it must be the Chest of Angry Blizzards on his betting slip.

A bit of time consulting the sidebar on the right of the screen revealed which Viking squads were which. Team

Ptool was green, Team Splatter was purple, and Team Burlap was blue. The blue Vikings were closer to the vaguely chest-looking icon and making rapid progress.

Mister Lewis glanced down and double-checked his slip. He definitely had money on the green Vikings. He glanced up at The Billionaire... who was smiling way too broadly for someone about to lose money.

He looked back at the screen. The blue Vikings had stopped moving. And then they started moving backwards.

The Billionaire's head was now nodding with the kind of enthusiasm usually reserved for an animated GIF on social media.

Now the purple Vikings were closing in, but the blue Vikings were blocking their way.

This didn't seem normal and the grumbling that was becoming increasingly loud in the betting room made it seem like something was amiss.

Mister Lewis slipped out of the room and made the short walk back to the theater. The spectators in the theater weren't grumbling, they were screaming. And the spectators weren't the only ones screaming. One cluster of players on the stage seemed on the verge of getting up and slapping another cluster of players who... looked intoxicated and unaware of their surroundings?

The other two teams on the stage seemed to be ignoring the noise and playing on.

Glancing up at the screen, the green Vikings were chopping their way through zombies in a wide arc around where the blue and purple Vikings were caught in a vicious knot of a skirmish. The purple Vikings were swinging their katanas at the blue Vikings, and the blue

Vikings were dying, but it was slowing the purple Vikings down to a crawl.

Mister Lewis reached into his pocket for his monocle, held it to his eye and scanned the stage.

Yes, there was a reason the blue Vikings had stopped advancing on the chest and the players piloting them in the real world looked dazed. Team Burlap was enveloped by a hex.

The theater crowd erupted in a mix of cheers, jeers and mostly disgust.

Looking up at the screen, the green Vikings reached what must have been the chest and won the game.

Looking back at the stage, the team controlling the blue Vikings were becoming aware of their surroundings again and the view of them through the monocle was significantly less interesting than it had been a moment prior.

Chapter Sixteen

Customer Satisfaction

B ack in the betting room, The Billionaire cashed in the winning betting slip without speaking a word to The Ticket Writer. Just a knowing smirk which was matched by an insincere smile from inside the betting window.

A discrete glance through the monocle still showed nothing unusual about The Billionaire, but why would it when the deed had passed?

"A word, if you please," a figure in a garish suit slid up aside The Billionaire.

The Billionaire glanced over but did not speak.

"A word about some coins," the figure continued.

The Billionaire replied with a head tilt and a frown, which was more attention than most people in the building seem to have gotten.

Mister Lewis paused just inside the doorway to the betting room. It didn't seem like a good thing The Billionaire was getting confronted immediately after the players had been hexed. Whatever did the hexing probably wasn't too far away.

"Yes, we know all about how you own the server," the figure's voice raised an octave. "You just cashed in your ticket over at that betting window. Some of us would like to cash in our tickets, too. Is this going to be a civil conversation or do I need to make a scene?"

"Perhaps outside would be best," The Billionaire's voice rumbled with irritation as an arm swept forth to point out the exit sign at the back of the room.

The figure nodded in assent and slipped out the back door, The Billionaire following close behind.

It took Mister Lewis a little longer than he'd have liked to weave through the crowd without causing too much of a scene. Ninety seconds later he was in the back corridor, rushing towards the exit. He reached for the bar on the door, only to quickly pull his hand back.

At least they hadn't cheaped out on the security door, that door must've been all metal, because at the temperatures it was radiating, a wooden door would've caught fire, instead of absorbing the heat on the outside and heating the inside like it was a hot stove.

He kicked at the bar and the door flew open. Fortunately, there was nothing blazing in the alley when the door opened. As it fell shut, he kicked it open again and darted through before it could brush against him.

What he found was all too familiar. Scorch marks in a vaguely human shape lay on the back wall of the building. Bits of detritus at the far end of the alley that hadn't quite finished burning yet either. Whatever produced that heat had some range to it.

Something was different this time, though. He almost missed it, but over the crackle of embers was another sound that was rapidly fading away like... the flapping of wings? He looked up and saw nothing, but the building was blocking much of his view. He ran out of the alley to the street and scanned the skies, but nothing was there, and the flapping noise was no longer audible.

Mister Lewis frowned and returned to the alley. One of the many problems with that kind of heat was it tended to sterilize the scene of the incident. He was done here. Or was he?

He approached the back door, realized it was still far too hot to touch and doubled back to the front.

"This is a winner?" Mister Lewis asked as he slid his betting slip into the window.

"Didn't I say you were following a winner's bet?" The Ticket Writer said with a smirk.

"Those must've been good odds," said Mr. Lewis as The Ticket Writer counted out twenty-dollar bills. "Was that not a popular bet?"

"The underdog was not getting much action today, no."

"So, when your boss won the bet, the book won, too?"

"Who exactly are you again?" The Ticket Writer slid a neat stack of bills through the window.

"Just a low roller looking for an angle. I appreciate the tip."

He slid a twenty back through the window and left.

Chapter Seventeen

The Invisible Hand Theory of Financial Holdings

"The Hippie may be right," Mister Lewis sat in The Head of HR's office. "For as much as these things sound like a random string of conspiracy theories, there's cause for concern. When I followed the trail from the second assassination attempt, I found a scorch mark where there used to be a body. When I went sniffing around where your Billionaire's front company was playing stock market games, more scorch marks turned up. When I went to observe your Billionaire in the flesh, sure enough, another body gone to ash, and it was probably The Hippie's friend."

"Let's get this over with then," replied the Head of HR. "What are your next steps?"

"There are competing theories of what to do in a situation where you have strong circumstantial evidence on a suspect. One theory is to apply pressure. Rattle them and see what happens, hope they slip up. The other is to hang back and observe. Gather more information and see how much of the operation you can figure out before they realize they're being watched."

"If there have been hit attempts, doesn't that already suggest an awareness of our activities?"

"The assumption that seems reasonable is that The Billionaire is aware of The Hippie's loud and public questions. And, obviously, the questions The Hippie's crypto associate tried to ask before winding up as a pile of ashes would be a tip off that people are talking. However, there didn't seem to be a reaction to my being in the same room at the eSports event, though. Maybe I'm too far down the food chain to be noticed and, then again, maybe we're just dealing with a cool customer."

"But you've determined that magic is at work here?"

"The eSports team was definitely ensorcelled. It was match fixing, pure and simple, just like doping a boxer's water bottle. And then whatever burned those bodies is most likely magical in nature or it would make a lot more noise and wouldn't vanish so quickly. There's no question that magic is showing up at every turn. I've encountered two demons. The problem is, we don't know who or what is casting the spells."

"Given The Billionaire has already been approached once with questions about that crypto coin, is it even possible for you to continue surveillance without pressure being applied?" asked The Head of HR. "It sounds like that's happening, regardless of anything you do."

"We have a 'known unknown' problem with all the magic floating around and that's going to dictate the next step," Mister Lewis said with a frown. "Direct agitation is a bad idea if I don't understand what's causing people to get cremated in alleys. There are already too many bodies getting cremated, and it won't do anybody any good if I end up as the next one. Observation is the better plan, at least until I have a better handle on exactly what kind of artillery is in play. Preferably with a little more distance between myself and the primary subject, lest I start getting recognized. What can you tell me about the rest of the business holdings? I don't necessarily have to be in the same room as The Billionaire to check up on things."

"The company would prefer a swift resolution to the situation, but If that's what you think is best..." The Head of HR opened a drawer, produced a folder and opened it on the desk. "The Billionaire has a string of holdings that neither our lawyers or The Hippie's friends have been able to identify. The charitable view would be to call them diversified holdings. The primary revenue stream comes from a palladium mine in Guatemala."

"You'd mentioned that," Mister Lewis's frown deepened. "I've never heard of Guatemala being a major center for palladium. Nickel, sure, but not that."

"It doesn't seem to be for anyone else. There is a string of offshore financial holding companies where ownership is... better classified as 'likely,' than concretely established as fact. The directly-owned, domestic holdings we can confirm are smaller and more eclectic. Two auto repair shops. A pawn shop. A numismatic collectables shop."

"A coin shop? As in physical coins, not the crypto coins that started this mess?"

"Antique and collectible physical coins," clarified The Head of HR. "I thought that was a little too cute to be a coincidence, as well. Schatzhorde des Drachen, the cryptocurrency entity, is offshore. We're still unable to tell who really owns it. That's all from The Hippie's sources."

"And The Hippie's intel has been close enough for horse shoes and hand grenades," Mister Lewis sighed. "OK, let's say I don't want to push my luck about getting noticed, how many of these holdings and alleged holdings are The Billionaire known to frequent?"

"The numismatic collectables shop seems to be more hands on than the rest. There has been the odd sighting at the pawn shop, but the auto shops don't seem to get any visits."

"The Hippie's friends have been staking those places out, have they?"

"As you said," The Head of HR nodded, "their intel has been more reliable than you'd expect. Take it for what it is."

"Then it's time to see if there's a relation between fixing cars and fixing bets," sighed Mister Lewis. "Or at least if there's anything supernatural around the garages. Sometimes a cigar is just a cigar, but this has been a series of 'high coincidence' events, and I wouldn't expect that to change."

Chapter Eighteen
Flashes of Suspicion

If nothing else, he could confirm the building at least looked like an auto repair shop. The sign that said "Auto Repair" was the first clue. The second clue was underneath the sign: a garage style overhead door with the sidewalk sloping down to the street to let cars drive in without having to jump the curb.

Mister Lewis crossed the street for a closer look. A slow stroll past the front door showed an unattended counter. A few steps later he passed the garage door. Sure enough, a turn of the head and a quick glance revealed there were mechanics bent over open hoods and at least one on a dolly underneath a car. The business of automotive repair was being conducted and that hadn't been a given.

Once past the building he started to turn into the alley next to it when a door opened, causing him to hop to the other side of the alley entrance and pause in front of the neighboring building. After a second, he glanced down the alley. A side door to the repair shop was swinging shut. That wasn't unusual. The unusual thing was what was strolling down towards the opposite end of the alley. Two people in ankle length trench coats with black fedora hats pulled down tight. The figures appeared to be about three feet tall.

Mister Lewis pulled his head back, trying to remember which film the scene reminded him of more: *Phantasm*, *Don't Look Now*, or *Bugsy Malone*.

He stuck his head back around the corner in time to catch the trenched up figures exiting the alley and hanging a left. He hurried through the alley a little too quickly for a leisurely stroll.

The racewalking chase continued for four blocks into a residential neighborhood, Mister Lewis doing his best to stay at least a half block and a corner turn behind. The chase ended with the figures in the street, heads tilted towards the ground, examining the frame of a Ford Mustang sports car. He took shelter behind a tree as the scene played out.

"I don't see any F-150's around here," said the first figure with a booming Scottish accent.

"That voice crosses Bugsy Malone off the list," thought Mister Lewis.

"We can get more for an F-250," said the second figure with a nasally English accent.

"Not like there are any of those around, either" scoffed the first figure, kneeling to stick a hand under the car. "The frame's too low. I'm going to have to crawl under. Hold my coat."

The figure took off his fedora, handing it to the second figure and revealing a melon-shaped bald head, a nose the size and shape of a large, narrow cucumber and a pair of googly eyes.

"A gremlin?!?" sputtered Mister Lewis under his breath. "A goofy *Phantasm* it is, then."

The Gremlin flapped open the trench coat, exactly like a flasher would. Fortunately, this revealed a well-worn flight suit, instead of something else that resembled a cucumber. He then shrugged off the coat and tossed it to the second figure, laid on his back and scooted underneath the Mustang.

"I think my scissors are in the coat pocket?" the brogue bellowed, and he stuck a hand out from under the car.

The second figure stuck a hand in the coat and slowly pulled out a shimmering pair of scissors that were longer than either figure was tall. It stuck the point of the scissors in The Gremlin's hand.

"The other way, you idiot," screamed The Gremlin.

The figure then put one of the handles into The Gremlin's hand. The scissors were drawn under the car and two unnaturally loud snips were heard. Then the scissors were tossed back out and The Gremlin crawled back into the light, a severed catalytic converter balanced upon his right hand.

While The Gremlin was preoccupied with retrieving his coat, Mister Lewis took the opportunity to retreat around the corner of the block.

"I suppose sabotaging cars isn't so different than sabotaging planes," The Gremlin muttered to himself. "That's still the work of a disgruntled mechanic."

"I don't find this satisfying," moaned the second trench coated figure.

"It's still a transport," replied The First Gremlin, starting to retrace his route back to the garage. "It's still sabotage."

"But it will still run without a converter. There's no crash. Where's the fun if there's not a crash?"

"Think of it as bounty hunting. That's exciting! And getting paid is exciting. We shouldn't be a charity."

"If you can't embrace the holy work that should be at the center of our lives, at least have some professional pride. Is there more pride in making an engine sound louder than in causing a crash?"

"When you make something crash, you make a very loud sound," said The First Gremlin with a sigh. "Look, a few more of these and we'll hop a flight home and haunt a proper airbase. But let's have a little more coin in the purse before we return, eh?"

The second figure didn't respond, so much as simmer.

As they neared the block the garage was on, Mister Lewis turned onto a side street to let them pass ahead of him. It wasn't exactly a mystery where they were heading. He wasn't sure if he bought either creature's argument over the other's. It was a strange scenario, but not necessarily much stranger than the week was already going.

Chapter Nineteen
Familiarity Breeds Consternation

It took twenty minutes to conduct their business inside the garage before the trenchcoated figures again exited the repair shop through the side door in the alley, without a catalytic converter in hand, but doubtless with cash in one of their pockets. No doubt, The Gremlin needed a little extra time to keep his partner calmed down while collecting his "bounty." What did Gremlins do with money, anyway? That had never really come up before.

At any rate, Mister Lewis was content to let them clear out before having a look inside the place. Whoever, or whatever, was running the shop was bound to get defensive if a stranger wandered in while "the help" were dropping off their prize and demanding recompense.

He doubled around the block from where he'd been lingering at the far side of the alley and walked straight in through the front door. There was no bell above the door to signal his entrance and even if there were, it probably wouldn't have been audible above the din of power tools coming from the maintenance shop floor.

He found himself in a waiting room. A few chairs, an end table with a stack of magazines old enough to make a dentist's office blush, and a door at the far end leading to where the action was. That door was slightly ajar. Pushing it open a bit further revealed more of what he'd seen through the open garage door: men bent over hoods or underneath chassis.

He pressed through the door, and no one looked up. Nothing looked out of place on the shop floor, and it seemed unlikely The Gremlins had been conducting business where they could be seen from the street, so Mister Lewis ventured in further. And that's when he noticed the door at the back of the shop. It was half open and metal glinted in the half-lit room behind it.

"Who are you?" came a snarling voice from behind him.

Mister Lewis ignored the voice and walked towards the door.

"Hey, I'm talking to you," continued the voice.

He approached the door. The backroom was filled with stray catalytic converters in varying states of repair strewn across the room. Then an arm shot over his shoulder and the door slammed shut.

"The storage room is for employees only," came the voice as the arm that had slammed the door withdrew.

Turning, he saw the voice belonged to a man with a skin condition. A face with rough patches of scaly skin with a green tinge to them. A peculiar complexion that he'd seen before in the recent past.

"Are you the manager?" asked Mister Lewis.

"Yeah, I'm the manager," came the reply. "Is there something I can help you with?"

"Do you do emissions testing?"

"Sure," The Manager's eyes narrowed slightly and paused before speaking. "Is your car out front?"

Yes, that peculiar complexion was practically a mirror image of the Ophidia Trading Company manager, whose pet lizards started this chase.

"Oh, I wasn't sure if I should even move it. It's making an awful racket when I turn on the engine. And that's on top of the smell."

"Smells like the devil's fart, does it?" The Manager's sudden grin spoke more of opportunity than kindness.

"I was going to say sulfur, but... I see your point."

"We get quite a bit of that these days. Somebody probably swiped your catalytic converter. We can fix you up with a new one. Expensive, but not hard to fix."

"I don't suppose there's such a thing as used parts for that?" Mister Lewis feigned ignorance.

"Oh, you'd want to be careful about that. A lot of them have the VIN number of the original vehicle etched on them. One of them shows up on the wrong vehicle, you might have legal problems."

"Does anyone actually check that?"

"You might be surprised."

"Is there a way around that?" Mister Lewis pantomimed reaching into his jacket for a billfold.

"You ask an awful lot of questions," The Manager's eyes narrowed. "You sure you're not with the city?"

"I live in the city?" Mister Lewis had been looking at that particular shade of green tinted skin long enough to start having doubts if it was a human color.

"Are you here looking for Federal problems? Environmental problems?"

"Well, yes. The converters are there for the environment. That's fair."

The Manager paused, frowned and then turned back to address the mechanics.

"Looks like we've got a smart-ass in the shop," came the bellow. "Does anyone want to help me explain how always following the law is the best policy? You do like to follow the law, don't you, pal?"

The mechanics slowly started disengaging with their work. Men slid out from under cars and stood straight after being bent over their hoods. Nobody put down their tools and a small crowd started to form, everyone clutching a hammer, a screwdriver or a wrench. And it occurred to him that these men were a little too well-proportioned in their physiques. A little too cut to be real. Almost like he was being menaced by caricatures of muscleheads come to life.

And they were stewing for a fight.

That's when his phone rang.

"Hold that thought," Mister Lewis raised a finger with his right hand and snatched up his cell phone with his left.

The Manager stared blankly, apparently unused to being ignored.

"What's up?" Mister Lewis said into the phone.

"There's been more stock market activity," came the voice of The Head of HR.

"That sounds serious," Mister Lewis adopted an exaggerated look of concern and angled his head to give the glowering crowd a show.

"A press conference has been scheduled. We're all well aware of the patterns, so I've texted you the details."

"I'll be there directly," Mister Lewis replied with the solemnity of a pallbearer, before replacing the phone in his pocket. "Something has come up. Would it be alright if I brought my car around tomorrow for you to take a look at? It's a quick thing to replace, right?"

The Manager's mouth opened and moved a little, but no sounds cut through the cognitive dissonance.

"Right," continued Mister Lewis. "I'll see you tomorrow."

He thought his reaction to the phone call had sold the speed of his strides as he left the shop, but if he wasn't already conspicuous, a brawl wasn't going to improve his anonymity or insignificance.

Chapter Twenty
Nothing So Polite as a Podcast

"But it remains a classic example of cinema verité," concluded The Swede, snuggly tucked away in the increasingly bunker-like podcasting studio.

"And now back to the primary topic of discussion," cut in The Hippie.

"We have a primary topic of discussion?" The Swede asked with a quizzical tilt of the head.

"We've always meant to getting around to choosing a formal theme for the show."

"Didn't we originally have a formal theme when we started the podcast? Or did we just happen to talk about the same thing for a few weeks? Never mind. Go on then. Enlighten our audience. That way I can be the last to know."

"Listeners," The Hippie's tone was suitable for announcing a cure for cancer. "The most pressing concern facing our country is financial crime. And we're going to do our part to stamp it out."

"I thought we discussed light entertainments?" asked The Swede.

"There comes a time when you have to step up and do something patriotic!"

"Oh, look at you. You sound so grown up when you talk like that. And was there a particular crime you wanted everyone to be aware of? A fraud by any chance?"

"Absolutely!" The Hippie's face reddened ever so slightly. "We must guard against the heinous perpetrators of cryptocurrency fraud!"

"Cryptocurrency?" The Swede failed to suppress a giggle. "I thought we established that Schatzhorde des Drachen couldn't possibly be a currency if there was nowhere to spend it?"

"The Dragon's Treasure Hoard represents the greatest value in crypto coins known to mankind! We cannot be silent about how they're being held hostage!"

"Humanity might disagree with that but keep going. How are we going to shed more light on the circumstances of your being swindled?"

"It has come to our attention…"

"And who is this 'our' you refer to?" Interjected The Swede.

"The holders of those Dragon's Treasure Hoard coins. We talk, you know."

"So, you keep saying. And you all seem to think you have agency in the matter, too."

"We create our own agency," growled The Hippie. "It's not like certain people on this podcast are lending a helping hand."

"You be you. Now, what is it that's gotten your attention?"

"Thank you for so graciously allowing me to continue. It has come to our attention that there's some stock market fraud going on by the owner of the Schatzhorde des Drachen platform."

"Do not say the name!"

"I don't have to say the name. Our listeners can easily look it up on their own. The important thing is it has come to our attention that the owner of the platform is shorting shares of Leverterol!"

"Is that some sort of disease?" asked The Swede. "And how do you short a disease?"

"You're not far off," replied The Hippie. "It's a pharmaceutical company. In addition to not letting us sell our coins, there is stock market manipulation occurring!"

"To any lawyers listening, please note that I am not the one making accusations. You have proof of what you're saying?"

"It's all being done by a chain of holding companies."

"And you can prove that?"

"My heart knows I'm right."

The Swede facepalmed and sighed, but the sigh wasn't audible over the thunderclap as another sudden storm raged outside and managed to shake the studio, despite the fortifications that had been installed.

Chapter Twenty-One

The Aggro Conference

M ister Lewis entered the building, mingling with the assembled financial press corps. It wasn't so different from the last press conference he attended. The scent of blood was still in the air, but perhaps there was a little more anger floating around the room. The press seemed on edge, but the employees? The employees looked... constipated. That angry, clenched facial expression that suggests the face isn't the only thing that's clenched.

"Today," began the Leverterol Press Officer, "we're here to set the record straight. We understand there have been some unsavory reports in the media about in-fighting at corporate events."

That was understating the reports. The actual stories had been about fisticuffs in the office, ranging from a one-sided boxing match to a cubicle-clearing brawl. How they'd managed to avoid having the police involved was becoming the subject of gossip. Questions about the company's culture were starting to be raised by the evening news. This led to those kinds of culture questions starting to trickle into the financial press, at which point management started to care a little more about culture.

"We are one big happy family," continued The Press Officer. "There is no malice in the boardroom."

The collective facial expression of the media in attendance was similar to a New Yorker viewing the "clearance sale" sign in the window of a Times Square shop that had been running the same sale for 15 years straight, although perhaps slightly less engaged.

"How about malice in the breakroom?" Called a voice from the back of the room.

"I'm not sure what you're referring to," The Press Officer's reply came with a slowly developing frown.

"How about cubicle walls getting knocked down by thrown chairs?" Called another voice in the crowd.

"We have been considering a move to an open office plan, if that's what you're referring to."

That was when the shoving started. An employee at the front of the room, behind The Press Officer, nudged another employee, shoulder to shoulder. The second employee responded by shoving back with an elbow.

"We have much more interesting news about some new products," The Press Officer attempted to change the subject.

The first employee retaliated with a two-handed shove. The second employee staggered back a step, barely keeping balance.

That's when a murmur started in the crowd of media.

"We are seeking FDA approval," The Press Officer attempted to reassert control, only to be knocked through the podium and into a pile on the floor by the first employee, who'd been launched by the second employee as the shoving match escalated.

Before either could get to their feet, their pile was lit up by a dozen flashes as the quicker members of the media had already begun snapping photos. Anyone who'd been shooting with a wide angle could've gotten a striking image of the second employee flexing and growling at the pile of co-workers.

The door to the cubicle farm burst open and a cluster of wild-eyed Leverterol employees charged out to gang tackle the second employee. The brawl was on.

Almost as a whole, the media started backing up as the fists started flying. Oh, nobody was ready to leave just yet. "If it bleeds, it leads," rules were in effect as the first bloody nose was painfully obvious and everyone was trying their best to frame a prize-winning photo of such a moving, if pummeled, subject.

The Press Officer made an ill-advised attempt at breaking up the fight and was rewarded with a Glasgow Kiss for his trouble. It was probably the fourth bloody nose by then, but the photo of The Press Officer's head snapping back as blood sprayed into the air proved to be the most lasting image of the event, eventually becoming a minor meme on social media. It would leave The Press Officer with an unusually personal damage control assignment piled on top of physical damage.

After about 5 minutes, security showed up. The main difference between Leverterol security and Leverterol employees was that security had steel batons and didn't seem angry as they hit people. No, security was sporting broad smiles as they clubbed the staff and separated the amateur pugilists and wrestlers.

Mister Lewis figured it would be no more than 10 minutes before traders started to hear about the scene and the stock would start taking a nosedive. It wasn't quite the same as the last stock manipulation scheme he'd run into. This was a variation on a theme, though, and there was precious little doubt it would prove just as effective for the day or two needed to cash in on the short. Still, if the presence of a succubus at the scene of the last financial crime was a coincidence, then this could be happenstance and he had yet to prove enemy action. For all he could prove, The Billionaire might just be benefiting from the real instigator's stock tips. Perhaps insider tips, perhaps not. Which brought him back to the real questions at hand: why was the room so thick with rage and what really caused the brawl?

Security had just about finished breaking up the fight, much to the disappointment of the assembled media. The Press Officer's nose was no longer spraying blood. It was down to an ooze, which wasn't quite interesting enough for continued photography. The Press Officer staggered back to the podium, intent on resuming the presser and attempting a final positive spin, but it was a little late for that. The media was disassembling, intent on filing the stories that would follow up on their initial spurt of social media hot takes.

The Press Officer frowned and retreated to the men's room to wash off his face and see what horrors the mirror would reveal about the past few minutes. Mister Lewis watched him tromp off with morbid curiosity.

The bathroom door started to swing shut, only to pop back open as the janitor exited. The janitor looked irritated. Not quite as irritated as the brawling employees had looked but irritated enough. The janitor stared down at hands stained with a shockingly bright, nearly neon blue as those hands pushed a mop bucket filled with water covered by a shimmering film of an even brighter shade of neon blue. The color seemed vaguely familiar, but he couldn't quite place it.

Chapter Twenty-Two

Probing

The first thing Mister Lewis noticed upon entering the bathroom was the pile of bloody paper towels topping off the overflowing trash can. The second thing he noticed was The Press Officer standing over the sink, dabbing at his still bleeding nose with a wet paper towel and casting a thousand-yard stare into the mirror. The third thing he noticed was a streak of neon blue on the counter in front of the sink next to The Press Officer.

"I think it's time we met," Mister Lewis extended a business card.

"I think maybe I've heard of you," The Press Officer glanced down at the card, but made no effort to pick it up. "You work with the recording industry?"

"Occasionally," replied Mister Lewis. "You understand why I'm here, then?"

"There's not much about today I do understand, but if you're who I think you are, you're here to tell me there's a good reason I don't."

"Were you aware your stock was shorted this morning?"

The press officer stopped dabbing at his nose. The frown deepened as he wadded up the paper towel in his fist and tossed it in the general direction of the trash.

"Who specifically shorted my stock?"

"A holding company called SerpensFiscus," replied Mister Lewis. "From a legal standpoint, I could only speculate who's behind it, but..."

"I know who they are. We wouldn't be the first stock they've shorted. It isn't that big a town. Some of us talk. SerpensFiscus is the harbinger of doom. Given your reputation, are you here to tell me that there was something... what's the phrase, 'unnatural' about that little display out there? Has SerpensFiscus been hexing everyone they've shorted?"

"All of it?" Mister Lewis paused to take a closer look at the blue smear by the sink. "I'm afraid I haven't been looking into things long enough to tell you how far this goes back. Let's just say it's looking like your difficulties might overlap with a problem another client has and the last stock shorting incident kicked off..."

"With an embarrassing display at a press conference. Yes, I know those folks. Are you telling me my CEO is in danger?"

"Maybe. Maybe not. That's been the pattern, but it's possible it's already over if they got what they wanted from that press conference."

"Let's be clear: are you saying that was planned?"

"For an incident to specifically happen today, while you were speaking? Things might not be planned out quite so precisely. It's more likely whoever's behind this has a window they're looking for unflattering headlines to surface in and those headlines have likely just started. If the stock dips enough, maybe they cash out. On the other hand, should that holding company get greedy... is your boss any good at boxing? That might even make the national evening news and cause an even bigger dip. For all intents and purposes, SerpensFiscus seems to be a hedge fund that operates on manufactured misadventure. Or at least that's the emerging pattern."

The conversation was interrupted by a string of tortured grunts emanating from the stall in the far corner.

"So, you're telling me I've got an alien on staff starting fights?" The Press Officer asked while looking nervously at the noisy stall. "That's what people in my circles have been saying about this 'pattern' of yours."

"An alien?" Mister Lewis cocked an eyebrow. "Well, if that's how they want to spin it in private, so be it. Let's simplify that to 'not human.' Maybe. Let's just say there's reason to be suspicious about the possibility of your company having been infiltrated by some flavor of outside instigator. We should probably take a close look at your recent hires. Might not be what's going on, but that's how some of this was started in the past and it's a good place to start. Off the top of your head, do you know anyone who sits next to people who've been in a fight, but that person hasn't participated in a throw-down? Within agitation distance, if you get my drift? We need to figure out how this spreads and that might help narrow it down."

"I'd have to ask HR, but at least a fifth of the company has been involved in one incident or another in the last week. This brawl was bigger, but tempers have been flaring all over the place for at least a week."

A scream came from the rear stall and the stall door rattled.

As he glanced over his shoulder to see what was rattling, Mister Lewis noticed a neon blue smear on the floor, spilling out from under the stall.

"Out of curiosity," asked Mister Lewis, "what's that blue substance on the floor over there? It seems like it's all over the place."

Before The Press Officer could answer, the stall door burst open, revealing a disheveled man in a suit with his shirt half untucked, his fly open and while his pants were buttoned, his belt was not buckled. The man's face was the personification of rage.

"If you wanted to ask HR, he can ans..." The Press Officer was interrupted when the angry man howled and charged them, arms out and hands opened wide, looking for a throat to grab.

Mister Lewis stepped into the charge and kicked the man in the groin. The air went out of him and he dropped to his knees, but he kept crawling forward, his hands darting out in a clawing motion.

Mr. Lewis kneed him on the chin and this time he stayed down.

"Is this guy new?" Mister Lewis gestured to the body on the floor.

"He's HR," replied The Press Officer, his face twisting into a grimace. "And he's also been here longer than I have. What's wrong with his pants?"

Indeed, there was something amiss about his pants. The pants were soaking wet over the buttocks and neon blue fluid was seeping through them onto the floor.

"Let's not touch that until we know what it is," Mister Lewis took a step backwards and checked his hands for stains. "Unless you were about to tell me what it is?"

"Nobody seems to know, but it's been showing up all over the place for a while. Whatever it is, it leaves stains that are supposedly hard to get out. That's not some kind of... diarrhea, is it?"

"I don't think so," Mister Lewis glanced at the trail of blue drops leading back to the far toilet stall. "Humans don't expel that color."

"I thought you said we were looking for someone who wasn't human?"

"I did," Mister Lewis stepped over the man from HR, took two more very tentative steps towards the final stall, kicked the door open and peered in.

There were more blue drops on the stall's floor. The toilet seat was smeared with more of the substance and blue-stained toilet paper floated in the bowl.

"But maybe that goo did come out of him?" Mister Lewis pressed the toilet's handle with his foot and the resulting flush cleared the bowl. "We better take a closer look at him."

As he started to step out of the stall, the sound of a tiny splash caught his attention and he turned to see something blue moving around in the toilet bowl. A neon blue slug was swimming around in the toilet.

"What in," began Mister Lewis, but he stopped in mid-sentence when the slug's optical tentacles tilted towards him.

"Back up towards the exit," Mister Lewis called to The Press Officer, while taking a step backwards, himself.

The slug seemed to rear back in the water and then shot out of the toilet at Mister Lewis, who dodged left. The slug bounced off the stall door, hit the floor and started crawling towards the bathroom entrance.

"Do not let it touch you," yelled Mister Lewis, his eyes darting around and settling on the polished gleam of a stainless-steel cylinder being used as a trash receptacle. He grabbed it and the remnants of paper towels spilled out as he brought it down over the slug.

"Was that the alien you were looking for?" asked The Press Officer.

Before he could answer, there was a squeaking noise and the slug slid out of the crack between the trash receptacle and the floor.

Mister Lewis stomped on it, which produced a squishing sound and splattered blue slime across the room.

"Not exactly an alien," said Mister Lewis, "but you can call it that if it's easier for you."

"You know what it is?" asked The Press Officer.

"It's called a Slug of Lyssa."

"Lyssa?"

"She was the Greek goddess of rage and madness. Goddess of rabies, too. I've never actually seen one of those before. They're very rare."

"And that's why there's slime in his pants?" The Press Officer glanced down at The HR Manager, still wriggling on the floor, and his soaked trousers.

"You saw how it navigated its way between the trash can and the floor? It's known to slip through anything that isn't sealed up tight. If those things are hiding in the toilet, we can make a pretty safe guess how they're entering the body."

"You mean it crawled up..."

"And died," interjected Mister Lewis. "That's where the saying comes from. Like I said, they're pets of the goddess of rage and rabies. And I'm probably going to need a new shoe. I don't think that blue stain is going to come off completely. But I suppose the next question is whether there are any more of them?"

He re-entered the final stall, paused and flushed the toilet again. The water went down. The bowl started to refill and as the water level rose, another slug squirted into the bowl with the rest of the water. Mister Lewis stuck his foot in the toilet and smeared the slug around the side of the bowl.

After removing his foot, he cautiously raised the lid on the toilet's tank and was greeted by the sight of a least a dozen more slugs floating above the flapper. He replaced the lid and sighed.

"I think I've identified your problem. Could you hand me some paper towels?"

The paper towels were handed. Mister Lewis rolled them into a wand, produced a lighter and lit one end of the towels. He then quickly flipped the lid off the toilet's tank and dropped the flaming paper towels into the tank. The slugs burned, crackling like a fireplace... except there was neither smoke nor a burning odor and the slugs below the waterline were also burning.

"How can you burn things underwater?" The Press Officer had stuck his head into the stall.

"That's a key difference between aliens and magic," replied Mister Lewis. "Magic has different rules. The lore says salt won't do anything to this kind of slug, but an open flame removes them from this plane of existence. That seems to check out, so if you've got any slime on you, keep it well away from the fire.

"Awfully convenient that you have gravity flush tanks in the public restroom. You do realize it's a lot harder to sneak these things into a toilet if you're using a commercial toilet? No tank."

"The one inside the office is that way," said The Press Officer. "I think it's only the lobby bathrooms that have tanks. You'd have to ask the building management offices why."

"Usually has something to do with the size of the pipes, but if the only tanks are out here, it would definitely explain why there weren't more people fighting."

The flames finished consuming the slugs, leaving the water in the tank looking clear.

"In theory, the fire consumes all traces of them," said Mister Lewis as he tapped the handle for a cleansing flush. "But if I were you, I'd probably have someone give it a good bleaching anyway."

The next stall's tank was empty, but the middle stall had nearly twice as many slugs as the final one.

"So... people don't actually use the middle?" asked Mister Lewis as the slugs crackled like a yule log.

"Or they were, you know, standing up," offered The Press Officer.

"Nah, same difference. Just don't try to visualize how that works. Is there a ladies' bathroom in the lobby?"

"Yes, but I don't think there have been any women getting into fights."

"Check it anyway. If somebody tainted this set of toilets, they could have tainted another."

"If somebody put them in the tanks, there are security cameras in the lobby. We can probably narrow down who did it."

"Here's the thing," sighed Mister Lewis. "Whatever's going on with the stock market, there may not be a human behind it. All the dirty work I've been running into? Hasn't seemed like very many humans were involved. Whatever planted those slugs... if it even shows up on a camera, it's not likely to show up in its natural form. You want to check, be my guest, but don't be shocked if nothing looks suspicious."

"What about the employees who were," The Press Officer groped for the right word. "Infected? Does this wear off?"

"You should probably give everyone two days off and it should be out of everyone's system. But if anyone gets in a dustup between now and then, tread carefully. The infection started in your building and it's possible you could have some liability."

"We don't like liability. And I would assume the stock shorting will be over soon?"

"That's the trend. I will, of course, be sending a bill for services rendered. And for a new pair of shoes."

Chapter Twenty-Three
One Man's Trash...

M ister Lewis paused to change his shoes and con-
template the chaotic string of events unspooling
around the attempted assassination of the podcasters.

His shoes were a total loss. There was a blue tinge
that wasn't coming out and, while there wasn't exactly
an odor, something made the back of his nostrils twitch.
It was odd, but it's not like many of the recent incidents
were governed by natural law.

He also wasn't entirely sure whether the slug's ability
to induce a state of rabid fury remained if there were still
traces of its color present or the contagion evaporated
as the ooze dried. If not, could it soak through the shoe
leather and enter him through his foot? Would it still
induce a state of rage if that discolored tip of the shoe
entered someone else's body through the same opening
the slugs had been penetrating?

It was easier to burn the shoes. He'd have to bill somebody for a new pair.

The phone rang.

"We've got a tip for you," said The Head of HR. "It
might be a stretch, though."

"More of The Hippie's friends?" asked Mister Lewis.

"Right the first time. They seem to think The Billionaire, through undetermined shell corporations, etc., etc., is now operating an electronics recycling shop."

"A shop? Do you mean a recycling facility?"

"Let's call it a storefront for the sake of simplicity."

"That's strange enough on its own," replied Mister Lewis. "Those things usually have to operate at scale, don't they?"

"And Legal can't determine that it's licensed," continued The Head of HR. "So, there's definitely something going on with it, just a question of what and whether it affects our situation."

"The Hippie's friends have a pretty good track record with this. Especially for a bunch of conspiracy theorists. It's worth a look. I assume this means there's no way to prove The Billionaire's involvement?"

"If it's on the level, it's possible something could be proven given enough time. That doesn't really operate on our schedule, though, does it?"

"It's not too late for me to have a look today," Mister Lewis glanced at his watch.

Chapter Twenty-Four

Low Overhead = Profit

T he sign on the building read "Electronics Recycling
Depositorium." The sign was new. The building
was not. In fact, the building looked like it might collapse
at any moment.

Mister Lewis glanced at his watch. The place should
be open for another fifteen minutes. Time enough for a
once over.

When the door opened, no bell rang. Then again, the
glass in the door was cracked and the hinges probably
squeaked enough to substitute for a bell. It wasn't so
much a case of nature providing as negligence bearing
fruit.

The door opened onto a largely empty room with a
front counter at the back of it. Behind the counter was a
ratty curtain that looked to be covering the entrance to
a back room.

And that was all there was to see. Nothing on the
counter. Nothing in the area in front of the counter.
Nothing on the walls. No merchandise. No security cameras. No security systems or anything that could possibly
conceal one. The only reason to think this wasn't an
abandoned building was the new sign out front and this

was definitely not what comes to mind when the sign outside says "electronics."

The curtain behind the counter rustled and shifted a bit, as though someone was in the back, so he stepped up to the counter and rapped on it. It turned out the counter was a decidedly chipped flavor of wood, and he almost got a splinter for his troubles.

The curtain parted enough to let a head through. A head with unkempt hair and particularly thick glasses which said "electronics" more than the décor did.

"Can I help you?" asked the head, which had a slight disembodied quality, sticking out through the curtains like that.

"Is this the recycling place?" Mister Lewis glanced around the room theatrically.

Those appeared to be the magic words, for the head popped through the curtain and now stood atop a slightly undeveloped body on the other side of the decaying counter.

"Oh, don't worry about the room. We don't keep anything out there. In this neighborhood? That would lead to a different kind of recycling. What did you bring for us?"

"Nothing today," replied Mister Lewis. "I wanted to make sure I was in the right place."

"You are, you are. But what do you have for us?"

"I was cleaning out my basement and I've got a few things that are old enough I'm not using them anymore."

"Go on."

"A couple old Walkman players."

"We can take those. Any computers? We really like to recycle computers."

"Well, yeah… there is a laptop I don't use anymore after the hard drive started acting funny."

"Oh, we get a lot of those. You should definitely bring that in."

The curtains in the back shook again and a voice called out.

"I don't see the rhodium."

That voice sounded familiar to Mister Lewis.

Then a shoulder parted the curtains. While the head was facing away, that nearly green shade of patchy skin was distinctive, and he did recognize the voice. The manager of the auto repair shop was in the back room.

"You know what?" Mister Lewis backed up a step. "I can bring the laptop in tomorrow. I should let you deal with that."

The auto repair shop manager was still facing towards the back of the shop as Mister Lewis turned to retreat. He was out the door in two steps.

"See you tomorrow," followed him out the door.

Chapter Twenty-Five
Backroom Dealings

M ister Lewis retreated a block and watched the store.

A "closed" sign appeared in the door five minutes earlier than the posted hours. Ten minutes later, a familiar figure exited through the door. The manager of the auto repair shop was toting an oversized alligator skin briefcase. Sometimes fashion-forward types would match a briefcase with their shoes. This was more an instance of the briefcase complimenting a facial complexion and it made for a slightly creepy effect.

The freak with the head followed five minutes later and locked up. Or what passed for locking up in a place like that.

Since the freak wasn't carrying anything on the way out, the alligator skin briefcase suggested either a delivery or a pick-up had occurred, therefore the back of the shop was undoubtedly the more interesting for sightseeing than the front. And if the bagman came from The Billionaire's auto repair shop, not only was this place likely to be hidden somewhere in the portfolio of holding companies, having a look around might even be illuminating.

He waited another fifteen minutes to be sure no one would be returning for a forgotten cell phone and approached the door. Unsurprisingly, it was not difficult to open.

The curtain parted to reveal a backroom that was and wasn't like the front of the shop. Oh, it was still little more than a firetrap that had yet to catch a spark, but there was at least some furniture back there.

The middle of the room was taken up by a rickety table and some sort of amateur chemistry set. The back wall was a shelving unit with a few jars that looked empty.

To the right was another table with computer equipment on it and to the left was... junk.

He went back to the shelf first. The jars were labelled: gold, platinum, silver, palladium and rhodium. The jars were also as empty as they had looked from across the room.

Moving over to the junk piles, a closer examination revealed it to be pieces of partially disassembled electronics. He picked up what used to be a computer hard drive and examined it. Pieces had been cut off it. The platinum and the gold bits, specifically.

He glanced back at the labels on the empty jars and then back to the pile. If a device came in a case, the case was cracked open, and it was lying in pieces. Fragments of circuit boards that have been broken up littered the floor and added volume to the piles.

He walked over to the table in the middle of the room and noted a series of large beakers with pieces of circuit boards in them and filled with clear liquid. The further down the row, the darker the shade of the liquid. He glanced at the bottles next to the row of beakers. One said "HCl" and the other, "H_2O_2." hydrochloric acid and hydrogen peroxide.

At least that made a little more sense. If there were coffee filters around, that is, and sure enough there was a half full box of coffee filters at the edge of the table.

That was a basic gold titration. Dissolve the boards in acid and peroxide for a few days and filter out the gold. It wasn't particularly fancy or quick, but it worked. You could repeat a similar process for other metals, but it was slow and a really inefficient way to do things.

He went back to the shelf. No, no more containers besides the jars and nothing was marked copper. Copper was the most common element to be recycled, but it was being ignored while high school science lab titration experiments were being conducted to extract gold?

Weird.

The piles of discarded components suggested they were just abandoning the copper, so there was no way this could be legitimate recycling. Nor could extracting trace amounts of the fancier elements be profitable. Even if this building was condemned and the shop was squatting without rent, it couldn't justify the man hours.

Then again, how much of this case had made sense, so far?

He crossed over to look at the computer table. Upon closer examination, it had 5 hard drives in external cases plugged into a hub and connected to the computer with a USB cable. An unusual setup, to say the least. Not the most efficient way to do anything, but since the drives were humming, it seemed like it was something set to run overnight, and speed was not necessarily the first priority.

He tapped the spacebar on the keyboard and the screen popped on. Sure enough, a data recovery program was being run on all five drives. Not precisely what you'd call a best practice in the recycling business.

He checked the documents folder and found what he expected, although perhaps more clearly labelled. The hard drives were being restored, if necessary, and then being searched for financial records, social security numbers and identity information.

Basic chemistry on one side of the room and identity theft on the other. And threads of digital fraud continued to be spun in The Billionaire's wake.

This presented something of a dilemma. While this was the first hard evidence of crime, especially crime that wasn't complicated by a supernatural element that law enforcement wouldn't recognize, it wasn't clear whether this could be directly tied to The Billionaire. Possibly, not even the manager of the auto repair shop, depending on how an official investigation went. Mister Lewis could already see two cutouts and the paperwork was obfuscated. Beyond that, legally investigating these things took time. Time he wasn't sure he had when it looked like someone was still trying to do in his client.

Still, he really couldn't let something like this go unchecked. Perhaps this was an opportunity to turn up the heat without having to show his face?

He returned to the low rent chemistry lab. Hydrochloric acid didn't burn. Hydrogen Peroxide, despite being rocket fuel, didn't technically combust, just explode. Coffee filters would burn, though.

He plucked a fistful of coffee filters and left a trail of them across the floor to the computer desk. Next, he picked up the computer's power cord, plucked a pocket knife from his pocket and cut a divot in the plastic casing, down to the wire. Then, he pulled a bit of the casing away by hand, better exposing the wire and obscuring the clean cuts of the knife. He didn't think it would necessarily convince a fire marshal that a rodent had been chewing on the wire, but a little ambiguity would go a long way towards rattling The Billionaire's cage.

He then set the cord down on top of a small stack of coffee filters, the exposed wire touching the filters. Then he waited. The first filter ignited, but that was expected. The trail of filters to the table with the chemistry set ignited. That, too, was expected.

The leg of the table did not ignite, but that dry and rickety floor did and that was even better.

Mister Lewis wasted no time in exiting the building. As he was crossing the street, he heard a muffled boom that suggested the chemistry table had eventually found its flames.

Chapter Twenty-Six
The Referral

T he phone rang.

"A mutual acquaintance referred me," said the voice on the other side. "Someone you recently met in a bathroom. I might have a similar problem."

"Been having fights in the office?" asked Mister Lewis.

"Nothing like that, yet... but my employer just got shorted by SerpensFiscus. We are keenly aware what kind of trouble has been following that holding company around. Are you available for an engagement?"

Chapter Twenty-Seven

When the Market Gives You Lemons

"I can't even begin to understand why we'd be singled out to be shorted," began The Head of Security. "Our stock's flying on merger rumors. Our balance sheet is solid. But I know what's happened to everyone else."

"A healthy stock has further to fall," replied Mister Lewis. "That's potentially more money to whoever's behind this. Try not to take it personally. This has all the earmarks of just being business to someone. Poisonous business, but business."

"It's my business to take this personally and I'd like to take it a step further. I have the means to fight back."

"Do you, now?"

"That's right," The Head of Security's smile had a cruel quality to it. "Those merger rumors are mostly true. I say mostly because it's a better deal than what's getting floated. We announce what the deal actually is, the stock's going up further and whoever's shorting is going to lose their shirt. Unless..."

"Unless they've got a plan for making sure the stock doesn't go up."

"And that seems to be what's happened every other time that holding company's name has come up."

"And if we can head off their plan," began Mister Lewis, "you can run a squeeze on the stock."

"Me?" The Head of Security feigned innocence. "I don't need to do anything at that point. The real announcement will drive the day traders crazy. They'll drive the stock up some more and the squeeze will take care of itself. I just want the pleasure of sitting back and watching the market bleed whoever's been pulling this crap. But first, I need to know how they're planning on undermining the stock. If we can spike that, then nature can take its course."

"Alright, first things first. Have there been any new employee hires in the last month or so?"

"No."

"Temps?"

"Not even temps. Everyone's been here at least six months. Changes are for after a merger, not before."

"That's interesting," Mister Lewis frowned. "There's a couple angles the surprise could be coming from and I've run into both with this scam. Could be there's an external force that's about to be applied... like that bathroom incident you heard about. Could be there's some long-term planning for hitting you and a mole's been here longer than at their previous spots. Perhaps you should show me around the office? Maybe we get lucky, and I'll see something that's off."

They left The Head of Security's office and meandered through the cubicle farm. Mister Lewis had fished his monocle out of his pocket and periodically brought it up to his eye to scan the room. All seemed normal for five minutes until he stopped and pointed.

"That one over there? Is that your last hire, from six months ago?"

"No," The Head of Security raised an eyebrow. "That's our Communications Manager. Probably been here ten years? Not recent at all. Why?"

"Oh, that's not good," replied Mister Lewis. "Something's happened to your Communications Manager, then."

"What are you talking about?"

"That's a Changeling and they don't typically hang around for a decade."

"You mean like elves stealing babies and leaving another elf behind?"

"Fairies, not elves. But that's not a fairy Changeling we're looking at. Probably Fae magic, though."

He held the monocle up and gestured for The Head of Security to peer through it. The view through the monocle showed a moldy log with sticks where the limbs should have been, moving as though it was human.

The Head of Security's mouth opened, then shut without speaking before leading Mister Lewis to an empty conference room.

"I was warned there might be freaky stuff involved," The Head of Security said with a slight groan. "How does that thing talk?"

"Let's give you another frame of reference," Mister Lewis adopted a placating voice. "You've seen The Six Million Dollar Man?"

The Head of Security nodded.

"You remember how the Robot Maker would replace people with robots?"

"You mean like the Fembots?"

"That was a different mad scientist, but basically the same thing. This is sort of the magic version of robotic impersonation."

"The log is a robot?"

"The log has been enchanted to move around, talk and, in general, impersonate the victim. It's not alive, it's just a thing that looks like your Communications Manager. If you think of it as a magic robot, that's close enough for practical purposes."

"So, there's been... an abduction?"

"Most likely," Mister Lewis nodded. "That's how it usually works with kids. Adults? Adults aren't the usual fare. Could be an abduction, could be worse. Which one is the Communication Manager's office? I'm going to need you to invent some pretext to lure them into one of the conference rooms for a 'serious' chat, so I can have a look around that office. See if there's a clue to how long this has been going on and how they're planning to torpedo your stock."

"Is it likely to get violent?"

"Not if you don't make the first move. Chances are, it will be most concerned with blending in, maintaining its assumed identity and completing its mission. It's when the plan's been executed, they might care less about causing a scene on the way out."

"Like one of those robots on TV."

"Exactly."

Chapter Twenty-Eight
The Off-Script Script

T he Communication Manager's office was entirely too neat to be occupied by a creative worker. Did that mean the Changeling had been in place long enough to rearrange the office or was the real Communications Manager a little on the stiff side? It was hard to walk in cold and tell.

On the other hand, it did make it a little easier to search the desk. Alas, nothing in the desk was particularly interesting... which was a vote for "stiff."

Tapping the keyboard brought the computer screen to life. Come to find out, the computer screen was a lot more interesting than the contents of the desk. The screen flickered onto a word processing program and a draft of an announcement. An announcement about a merger falling through. An announcement with atrocious spelling and grammar. It would seem Changelings didn't know how to use spellcheck.

He clicked the print button, but when he turned to the printer, he found the announcement already in the printer tray as a second copy started to spit out. Was a third copy floating around somewhere? It seemed like the wheels of sabotage were definitely in motion, but it wasn't clear how many rotations they'd made.

When Mister Lewis entered the conference room, the faux-Communications Manager was spitting up a veritable buzzword bingo card while trying to explain the rollout schedule for the merger announcement. There were a lot more acronyms being thrown around than dates.

"The general idea," said the faux-Communications Manager, "is to create fear of missing out amongst the day trading community, which should cause them to be bullish on the stock. If we can get them bullish enough to keep the upward trajectory, some of the day trading may turn into swing trading and possibly into long side trading, although day traders do not typically have alignment with long side arrangements."

"So, you're proposing a strategic alignment with a proactive approach to cultivating the day trading community?" Mister Lewis was, after all, supposed to be a consultant. He felt it important to live up to that billing every once in a while.

"...the big picture idea," began the faux-Communications Manager after a pause, "is to engage in blue sky thinking with the day traders and create a win-win for both of us with an increase in stock prices."

"But what about the pain points?" asked Mister Lewis.

"Pain points?"

"Yes, there seems to be a disconnect between the pain points of the audience and putting this merger on the record."

"Pain points?" repeated the faux-Communications Manager.

"The day trader's pain point is a need for profit," Mister Lewis struck a stern pose. "The optics of the announcement must create a synergy and appear to mitigate risk for the trades. Does your announcement do that?"

The faux-Communications Manager stood unmoving and open mouthed.

"And you've already made the announcement?" asked Mister Lewis.

The faux-Communications Manager nodded no.

"Does this mean you're prioritizing a proactive timeline to empower the market to be proactive, not reactive, while unpacking the value and hitting the ground running?"

The faux-Communications Manager's mouth was still open, but no sounds emerged from it.

"Ah, I see I've exceeded your capacity for trade jargon?" Mister Lewis sighed as he handed the printout to The Head of Security. "Don't worry. It's really a second language, but I'm just not confident this press release meets all the requirements. Accuracy, most of all."

"That's not how you spell..." began The Head of Security before freezing up as blood and cold rage found their way to the face. After a brief pause to process conspiracy theories, questions were once more directed at the faux-Communications Manager. "If you didn't have a date in mind to announce the merger, did you have a date in mind for when the merger would be cancelled?"

The faux-Communications Manager flashed a grin that was a little too wide to be natural and paired it with a shoulder shrug.

"Perhaps you have access to information I don't?" asked The Head of Security, holding up the printout.

The faux-Communications Manager continued to grin without comment.

"What were you going to do with this?" asked The Head of Security. "An official press release? Hold a news conference? Leak it in emails?"

The faux-Communications Manager kept grinning.

"Is it already leaked?"

The reply was that constant grin.

"The fixed smile of a marionette," muttered Mister Lewis as he stepped forward and slipped the printout out of The Head of Security's hand. "Since this obviously doesn't mean anything to you, you won't mind if I dispose of it."

The faux-Communications Manager tilted its head slightly without breaking expression.

Mister Lewis nodded his head slightly as he tightly rolled up the printout, fished a lighter out his pocket and lit the tip of the printout. Then he waived the burning paper under the faux-Communications Manager's nose.

The grin remained in place, but the rest of the Changeling flinched.

"No, I didn't think you'd like fire," Mister Lewis said before tossing the half burned down printout into a trash can. The rest of the trashcan ignited, and he pushed it in front of the Changeling with his foot. "If you don't want to get acquainted with a bigger fire, you can start by telling us where the real Communications Manager is."

The Changeling backed up against the wall but kept silent.

"You don't have an out," said Mister Lewis. "Bring the real one back. Now."

"It doesn't work that way," The Changeling finally spoke again.

"What doesn't work?"

"Threatening me. True, the Fae will sometimes return a mortal if their proxy is threatened. Alas, my master is not of the Fae and not so soft-hearted. You waste your breath."

"Who said I was making threats?" Mister Lewis nudged the burning trashcan an inch closer to the Changeling. "I have no intention of letting you leave if I'm not getting that hostage back. Some legends say the missing child returns if you burn the Changeling to ash. Does that apply to missing adults, too? I'm willing to test that if you don't give me another option."

The Changeling's smile turned upside down, but it was still a caricaturish exaggeration.

"What's it going to be?" Mister Lewis growled as he pushed the burning trashcan another inch closer.

The sound of metal hitting metal caused everyone to turn as a cart from the mailroom was clumsily forced through the conference room doorway.

"This room is occupied," said The Head of Security to the skinny youth pushing the cart.

The youth didn't reply verbally. Instead, an arm was raised and the hand at the end of the arm stretched and extruded until it rested in the shape of a mallet. Its texture, unsurprisingly for the room, looked like wood.

There were a lot of things going on in that room that The Head of Security didn't understand. Raising a mallet was a threatening gesture, though, and it didn't matter whether or not that mallet used to be a hand. Threats...

those were something The Head of Security knew how to deal with.

A right hook struck the youth squarely in the jaw. The youth did not flinch, and The Head of Security howled in pain.

"Remember," sighed Mister Lewis. "They're made of wood. It only looks like it's flesh."

The mallet-hand swung towards Mister Lewis, missed by a wide margin, and took a chunk out of the conference room's table.

The Head of Security put two hands on the youth and shoved. The youth careened into the wall and bounced off before hitting the floor.

Mister Lewis swung his head back to The Changeling he'd been interrogating. The grin had returned and both hands were now mallet heads, which were swinging at him. He threw himself sideways to the floor as the mallets took bigger chunks out of the table.

On the floor, he rolled to his back and swept a leg out to tangle up the Changeling's feet, causing the Changeling to fall forward onto the burning trashcan. The Changeling's clothes quickly caught fire and its mouth opened to scream, then froze as its body changed back to a log with sticks for limbs and then fell to the floor. The sticks that were its legs blazed and the log at its center smoldered.

"Looks like the spell is disrupted when the center mass starts to burn," Mister Lewis looked up to see The Head of Security pinning the second Changeling to what was left of the conference table by its arms. "Can you hold it there for a minute?"

"It's not as strong as you'd think when it doesn't have leverage," said The Head of Security. "It's kind of slippery though, so you might want to hurry."

Mister Lewis turned to the smoldering remains of the first Changeling and snapped off the stick that was its arm. He stuck the stick in the trashcan's flame and paused for it to ignite.

"Now would be good," The Head of Security called over.

The second Changeling's limbs had gone as limp as overcooked noodles. While The Head of Security still had it by the wrists, it was in danger of wriggling free.

Mister Lewis pulled out the burning stick, walked around the table and jabbed it into the second Changeling's back. Its mouth opened to scream and then it reverted back to a log and sticks, collapsing onto the table.

"I'm going to get a fire extinguisher," said The Head of Security as what remained of the conference table started to burn.

While waiting, Mister Lewis grabbed the first Changeling by what was left of its legs and swung it onto the table and into what was rapidly becoming a bonfire.

"It might be better to put out the smaller fires first," he said to the returning Head of Security. "Let the remains of the Changelings char a little more first. I don't think they're likely to reanimate, but why take chances?"

"Are there more of those things around here?" Asked The Head of Security.

"That remains to be seen. Was the second one supposed to be someone from the mail room?"

"That's right. Only person in the mail room, if that matters."

"I should probably have a look around over there. Was there another press release prepared for this merger? Somewhere you can lay hands on it? And is there somebody else who can send it? Whatever you do needs to happen before anyone figures out we found the plants."

"Was that a pun?" The Head of Security grimaced.

Mister Lewis shrugged his shoulders.

"If we're in a hurry," continued The Head of Security. "I'll just have it leaked. There are a couple finance bloggers with big mouths who won't even bother fact checking. That'll be faster."

Chapter Twenty-Nine

The Mailroom Always Slays Twice

M ister Lewis did not usually wear his monocle but did so on his trip to the mailroom. If there were more Changelings lurking among the staff, they were not the kind that trafficked in illusions and he wasn't seeing them.

The mail room itself did not necessarily seem unusual. It looked like perhaps two days' worth of mail was unsorted, but that wasn't necessarily a red flag, depending on the efficiency of the regular employees. All it did was establish a likely time frame for the mailroom Changeling having been inserted into the office.

No signs of blood. No signs of struggle. Just unsorted mail.

The back of the room opened onto the alley, presumably where the mail was delivered. He opened the door and stepped out. It was on the clean side for an alley. Again, nothing remarkable.

He strolled the length of the alley, turned and peered through the monocle. Nothing unusual.

He was about to re-enter the building when something on the alley wall opposite the door caught his attention. Traces of ash on the walls.

This wasn't the full scorched outlines he'd seen before. There was, however, what could have been the top of a head, part of a hand and a bit of a leg. Like someone had done a rushed and sloppy job of cleaning it up.

Now having a better idea what to look for, he ventured further into the alley. It only took a few steps to find was he was looking for. Right next to the back door were more fragments in soot. Like someone had been taken out back and put up against the wall.

Interestingly, the wall was still a little warm.

An inspection of the rest of the alley proved empty. However many Changelings were in play, it didn't look like the people they'd replaced had been kidnapped by Faeries. That hadn't been a lie. He supposed he shouldn't have been surprised by the scorch marks, either. They'd been around the periphery of previous incidents, but perhaps things were starting to escalate?

It took him a few minutes to find the Head of Security who was huddled over a computer with a junior-looking employee.

"You find anything?" asked The Head of Security.

"It's probable that two people were executed in the alley outside the mailroom," replied Mister Lewis.

"Are there bodies in the alley?" The Head of Security stood bolt upright.

"No, just scorch marks. When people go missing around these stock market games, they tend to be incinerated."

"How?"

"I'm working on that. What I know is, there are fragments of scorch marks consistent with what I've seen before in multiple places. Likely, your mail room clerk and the Communications Manager. The wall under the second set of marks is still warm, so I'm guessing that was the Communications Manager and it was done today."

"You figure they're both dead?" asked The Head of Security.

"You're going to have to play it like they've gone missing," sighed Mister Lewis. "If they have family, figure out a way to pay the death benefits early. Make it look like a goodwill gesture or something. There's not enough left for the police to find. I'm not seeing any more Changelings, but that doesn't mean something else hasn't been embedded here. Whoever's behind this doesn't seem shy about leaving damage behind."

"The leak is starting to spread," interrupted the junior employee.

"Does it usually take this long?" asked The Head of Security, peering down at the computer screen.

"There's more throttling on social media these days," replied the junior employee. "Fewer people see the first post, fewer people share it. This kind of insider information will still get around, it's just going to take a few minutes longer. Blame the owners of the networks."

"Never mind that," interrupted Mister Lewis. "Is it moving the stock the way you expected?"

"Give it a few minutes," said the Head of Security.

As they waited, someone new stuck their head in the office.

"You wanted to know if the Communications Manager's phone started ringing?"

"How many times?" asked The Head of Security.

"Seven, back-to-back."

"Blocked number?" asked The Head of Security.

"Every time."

"There weren't any cellphones on those bodies?" The Head of Security turned to Mister Lewis.

"The clothes were an illusion," replied Mister Lewis. "They had no pockets to keep a phone in. With that kind of magic, there are likely more direct lines of communication."

"Then whoever sent them has figured out something's gone wrong."

They waited a bit more and as predicted, the stock price began to rise on the rumors.

The Head of Security's phone rang.

"A certain holding company has initiated covering their short," announced The Head of Security after answering the phone. "They're exiting their position. I think it's over."

"They've definitely lost money, then?" asked Mister Lewis.

"Not as much as I'd like. They figured out something was wrong fairly quickly. But yeah, they're in for some red ink. Does this mean we got shorted by elves?"

"Probably not," Mister Lewis frowned. "The Changeling said it wasn't being run by the Fae. Whatever enchanted those logs was definitely using Fae magic, though. And that's not something humans are generally capable of."

"So, we were shorted by something inhuman, it just wasn't an elf?"

"More likely, you were shorted by a human. A human who hired something to cast that spell in much the way you hired me to clean up the spell's mess."

"Should I be worried about reprisals?"

"It's hard to say," said Mister Lewis. "I get the impression whoever's doing this doesn't like attention. On the other hand, this might be the first time they've actually lost money in the process, and you don't play these kinds of games if you don't like money."

"A definite maybe, eh?"

"It wouldn't be a bad idea to finish burning those logs."

Chapter Thirty

Pieces of a Different Puzzle

S earching the events of the last few days for causal links was a much less straightforward affair than replacing a shoe stained with rage-inducing slime.

So far, the assassination attempts on his clients had failed but another whistleblower had died as a group of "investors" tried to get to the bottom of a probable cryptocurrency scam The Billionaire was thought to be running... but, as with many things in the crypto world, the identity of who created the crypto coin and exchange in question was challenging to prove.

A series of supernaturally manipulated stock scandals ran parallel to the assassination attempts where The Billionaire was thought to be behind the holding companies shorting the stocks taking the profit... but could not yet be proved to be the owner.

The common thread between the assassination attempts and the stock scandals was a trail of bodies reduced to scorch marks and a scattering of ash by some kind of improbably powerful heat source. There was no question that deaths were being racked up.

There was the eSports equivalent of point shaving seemingly accomplished through mystical means... adjacent to a crypto coin whistleblower's apparent incineration. Circumstantial evidence at best, but where there's smoke there's fire... if he could just figure out what was generating that fire.

Then there were the Gremlins stealing catalytic converters and depositing them in an auto repair shop owned by The Billionaire. No financial crimes involved in that, at least not on the surface, but at least more of a direct link to The Billionaire, even if an absentee owner could claim ignorance of what went on in the building.

Still, that repair shop manager had turned up at the place pretending to recycle and there did appear to be actual financial crimes going on there... but at least two degrees of separation away from The Billionaire between wayward employees and holding company cutouts. Well, that and the evidence being up in smoke.

Nothing was really actionable in the short term and there was still the small problem of discovering what was incinerating those bodies and how to avoid falling victim to it.

He went back to the list of The Billionaire's confirmed assets. The next item was a pawn shop that had its own folder among the documents that had been provided. A rather peculiar pawn shop that styled itself more as jewelry store. A shop where pawn tickets were never redeemed, and gold seemed to fly off the shelves.

Well, perhaps "fly" was not the right word. If the research was accurate, "disappeared" might be more apt. What little gold stayed on those shelves usually ended up identified as stolen when the police made their rounds. Except most of the gold passing through that shop didn't stay on the shelves. Except, the gold that left shelves didn't show on the ledger as having been purchased, it just... disappeared.

Was the disappearing gold an example of shoplifters treating the place like they were in a loyalty program or was it a fiction dreamt up for insurance claims? If stolen gold was stolen a second time, did it become a double negative and stop being stolen? The police had very little confidence that the store's ledger bore much resemblance to reality. Gold appeared. Gold disappeared. And too much of it was hot. The shop would have had its license pulled and shut down several times over, were it not for the expensive lawyer its Billionaire owner kept on retainer. The sort of lawyer this sort of shop would never otherwise see.

He wondered where the Head of HR had lain hands on the police reports, but he had no room to talk about such things.

There was a jar labelled gold at the recycling storefront, so precious metals were starting to become a recurring theme with this case. At least the catalytic converters wouldn't be getting lonely.

Still, the police reports on the pawn shop were the only official link between The Billionaire and previously documented crimes, regardless of whether improprieties could be sloughed off on the shop's manager.

On the other hand, the pawn shop didn't have any supernatural activity reported around it... though the detectives of the Burglary Unit were unlikely to recognize such things.

Still, if something mundane like trafficking in stolen goods could be established, that might be enough to push The Billionaire into the criminal court system and perhaps take The Billionaire's presumed attention off his client. It was worth a look.

Chapter Thirty-One

Little Shoplifters of Horror

T he actual contents of the pawn shop were not quite as skewed towards jewelry as the police reports suggested. Oh, there was plenty of jewelry. That wasn't even a question. It took up most of the display case under the front counter.

Mister Lewis nodded at the manager behind that counter and headed towards the back of the store, passing a rack of $1 DVDs that a quick glance revealed were best not discussed in mixed company. He couldn't decide if Internet streaming had driven another store out of business or a collector had finally gone blind.

Reaching the back, he glanced up at the front. The manager was still there, attention returned to a desk behind the counter. The back of the shop was apparently the noise section. It contained an assortment of musical instruments with unusual dents that may or may not have come during friendly discussions about when loan payments were due. Some questionable stereo equipment decorated the back wall and a pile of CDs spilled into the middle of the sprawl.

He moved forward an aisle and discovered some of the gold referenced in the police report. It wasn't limited to jewelry, either. A set of golden goblets was displayed

on the middle shelf. A bit more ostentatious than its surroundings, but present. Next to it stood a golden statue
of Elvis Pressley, although Mister Lewis suspected it was
merely gold plated.

Come to think of it, "golden" was even in the title of
one of the DVDs.

He moved on to the next aisle and its collection of
crystal drinkware that made those goblets look modest
and tasteful, only to hear the sound of crashing metal springing forth from the gold aisle. When he stuck
his head back in the previous aisle, two of the golden
goblets were on the floor... and two more nowhere to
be seen. There was no sign of what had disturbed the
merchandise.

He frowned and moved forward another aisle, closer
to the front. This one contained a rack of gently used
shotguns. Unsurprisingly, the only clean areas of the
shotguns were the areas that fingertips might rest on. A
sure sign of a classy joint!

Reaching the edge of the aisle, he glanced towards
the front counter and saw something both familiar and
unexpected. The pawn shop's manager was in conversation with a very short person in a trench coat and a
hat that was pulled down. A familiar hat and trench coat
he'd last seen at a certain garage filled with "liberated"
catalytic converters.

Was that repair shop some kind of hub for The Billionaire's off the books activities?

The pawn shop manager ducked below the counter
and came up with an overstuffed bag half the size of
that trench coat, which proceeded to get stuffed inside
the trench coat without the slightest bulge showing.

Probably resting right next to a pair of giant scissors, he suspected.

Mister Lewis tried to get a little closer without being too conspicuous and advanced another aisle to stand behind a shelf of wrenches, drills and assorted hand saws, most of which had seen better days. And then more clanging of metal came from the back of the store. He retraced his steps back to the aisle of golden excess.

The aisle was not the same as he'd left it. The goblets that had fallen to the floor were no longer on the floor. Or back on the shelf, although anything that had been standing on the shelf had now fallen over in a state of disarray. Out of the corner of his eye, he caught a flash of movement at the end of the aisle. If he'd had any doubts, that confirmed it. He wasn't the only one in the back of the shop.

Cautiously, he approached the end of the aisle, peered around the corner, and discovered a second short, trenchcoated figure slipping the golden Elvis statue inside a trench coat that matched the one at the front of the store.

It was not entirely unexpected. One Gremlin made a pickup and the second Gremlin double-dipped while the manager was occupied.

As the first wrapped up business at the counter, the second slunk back towards the entrance. They arrived at the front door simultaneously, tipped their hats at each other and left together like they'd been performing some kind of dance. If it was as well-rehearsed a routine as it appeared, it would certainly explain those police reports.

Mister Lewis paused a moment to let them start their journey before he began the tail, although he had a hunch he knew where they'd be heading towards. "Parallel lines sometimes meet," he thought to himself.

Chapter Thirty-Two

The Philosophy of the Five Finger Discount

T he trench coats headed south in silence for two blocks. Predictably, they seemed to be heading in the general direction of the auto repair shop Mister Lewis had last seen them in.

"Quit sulking," said the one who'd taken the bag from the manager in a thick Scottish accent. "It's all over after tonight. This is the last job."

"Can we leave tonight?" asked the second one in a Brummie accent.

"That depends. Will you be content not to sabotage our flight until we're over home soil? How's your self-control tonight?"

"My self-control has always been perfect," the second one growled.

The first Gremlin stopped and turned to face his companion.

"Is it now?" he asked. "Perfect like when you pilfered more trinkets from the shop? Which is to say, pilfering from our esteemed employer? I thought we had discussed that and come to an agreement."

"Everybody steals from that place. And we don't photograph, remember? The manager didn't see me. Their sad attempts at a security system didn't see me. There is nothing to make anyone suspicious of... what do they call it over here? Employee theft? Besides, we deserve a bonus for all we do around here. And for keeping quiet about everything we know."

The first Gremlin's eyes were lost in the shadow cast by his hat, but there was no doubt he was glaring in response to his comrade's answer. He said nothing as he turned and continued walking south with a bit more stomp in his step.

"You want to fly out tomorrow?" asked the second Gremlin.

"If you can't control yourself, I think we should take a boat. I don't want to end up swimming back here every time we try to go home and that's only if you lose control and sabotage the plane while it's still close to shore. It would be just my luck if you decided to wreck us in the middle of the ocean."

"What? You mean stow away on a boat? How long would we have to be hiding down below before we got home? We're on the wrong side of the continent! That could take months!"

"It takes as long as it takes. And that's after we can find a boat making the trip. Otherwise, we might have to switch ships at the next port. Maybe a couple ports. But we might not have to stow away."

"You have a plan?"

"Yes. You can pay for us to stay in cabins out of the proceeds from what you've been stealing from our employer's pawn shop."

The second Gremlin jumped up and down violently enough for his hat to fall off and reveal his odd features.

"That is not why I've been collecting bonuses for us," he sputtered while replacing the hat.

"There is another option you might prefer," the first Gremlin's said with no small measure of malice.

"Yeah? And what's that, then?"

"We could wreck a couple planes over here. Wreck as many as we need to until you get those urges calmed down and you get some self-control back. Then we fly home."

"That is a better plan."

"You like any plan that lets you crash a plane tonight."

The two Gremlins nodded in agreement and walked the rest of the way to the auto repair shop in silence.

Chapter Thirty-Three

Now You're Cooking

T he Gremlins were bold enough to enter the auto repair shop through the front door. When they opened the door, they were challenged by one of the overly muscled mechanics that staffed the place, reminding Mister Lewis of the functional army that resided behind those walls. The front door was glass and there seemed to be a lookout stationed behind it, so he kept his distance and doubled around the block to approach from the far side of the alley that contained the back door.

The alley was empty and the door was closed. Mister Lewis took a tentative stroll down the alley, keeping close to the wall on the side the shop was on. All was quiet as he approached the overhead door, in marked contrast to what was transpiring inside the shop. Next to the side door was another overhead door for letting cars enter and exit the shop. Like its counterpart in the front, this overhead door had plexiglass panels at roughly five feet above the ground. Through the plexiglass, all he could see was overly wide backs and shoulders. The mechanics were near the door, and something was going on. He backed away quickly before anyone could see him and clung to the wall.

That was when the wall started to warm up.

It was a brick wall, nothing particularly special about it, but Mister Lewis had started to feel heat coming off the bricks through his clothes. Puzzled, he turned to face the wall and attempted to place a hand on it. It was now too hot to touch and while the alley didn't quite qualify as a sauna, the temperature was definitely rising.

Remembering the scorch marks of bodily remains that formed the connective tissue of this case, he ran out of the alley and turned the corner on the far side of the block.

Then he waited.

After a few minutes, he heard a faint hissing noise coming from the alley. He stuck his head around the corner and observed steam leaking out from around the edges of the overhead door, which apparently didn't have a particularly tight seal.

The steam stopped and then all was quiet again for perhaps 20 minutes. Then the unmistakable sound of a car door opening came from the alley. It was followed by the revving of an engine and seconds later, a bright yellow 1978 AMC Gremlin sped out of the alley, took a right and stopped at the end of a block for a red light.

Mister Lewis turned his head for a better look. The AMC Gremlin's shape was fairly distinctive among cars, but something seemed off about it. The lines of the car were at crisp right angles. It was almost too boxy to be a Gremlin. Like it was some foreign-made knock-off, although that's the last car anyone would have wanted to copy. Never mind that the coincidence was a little too cute to be real, given what he'd followed back to the repair shop. But if it wasn't a Gremlin, what was it?

He started to walk towards the corner to see who, or what, was driving the car. He was half expecting to see hats pulled down over the collars of trench coats. He'd almost gotten to the car's rear bumper when the light changed and the car took another right, giving him a profile view of the driver.

Now, that was unexpected. The Billionaire was behind the wheel. Granted, The Billionaire owned the shop, but it was not every day you saw someone with that kind of wealth driving anything that resembled a Gremlin.

Chapter Thirty-Four

The Color of Money

Mister Lewis got lucky again when he found a cab before the Gremlin was out of sight. With that particularly vivid shade of yellow, it was neither the hardest thing to follow or even the hardest thing to bribe a cab driver to follow. The cabbie didn't even demand an elaborate explanation, which was refreshing.

The only curious thing about tailing the car was how low to the ground it was riding for something that had just left a repair shop. Its undercarriage scraped the road a couple times as the car traversed the city's hills.

When the Gremlin turned into Pier 73, he got out of the cab and followed the rest of the way on foot. The nice thing about those piers was the mishmash of things you found lying around on them. Equipment someone couldn't be bothered to put away. Rotting fish that hadn't sold. That convenient cargo container Mister Lewis was able to duck behind when he spotted the Billionaire walking back towards the street.

Given that he still didn't know what was causing the scorch marks, he decided to leave The Billionaire alone and find out why that Gremlin looked so odd, so he headed deeper into the pier.

Eventually, he found the Gremlin parked near a line of sports cars queued up to be loaded onto a cargo ship. A little quick scouting placed the ship as nearing its return trip to Puerto Quetzal in Guatemala.

When he finally got a good look at the front of the car, Mister Lewis noticed something else was off with it. The Gremlin was sporting a Jaguar hood ornament. His brow wrinkled a bit as he traced the edge of the car's strangely squared off outline, only to find yellow paint on his finger.

A closer look revealed something white showing through where the paint had come off. A little more rubbing showed it was white metal, not white paint. Whatever this car was, it wasn't made of steel or iron, like you'd expect. But a white metal? Platinum?

He reached into his pocket and produced a pocketknife. Whatever it was, it wasn't scratching very easily. That probably eliminated platinum. But what did that leave? Palladium?

Oh. Palladium on a ship to Guatemala. Yes, that would explain a few things about The Billionaire.

He tried the car door. It opened and it was heavier than it should have been, but probably not platinum heavy. Yeah, definitely palladium.

"How many catalytic converters do they have in that place?" he muttered to himself, taking another look at the strange outline of the alleged Gremlin and thinking the car's dimensions were a little too big for a Gremlin. He couldn't tell if they'd laid palladium over the original car or if the car's body was an entirely new, and mostly wrong, fabrication. Either way that had to be more than a ton. A very expensive ton, too.

He moved up to the next nearest sports car on the pier. He wasn't sure of the exact model, but it vaguely resembled a Lotus, except its lines were also a little too squared off. The paint was dry, but he was able to pop the trunk and, sure enough, the lid was far heavier than it should have been.

Taking a longer look at the rest of the cars, he decided somebody must've been in a hurry when that Gremlin was modified. The rest of the cars in the lot were by no means perfect, but they at least required a second glance to wonder if something was off.

There didn't seem to be much of a point in checking more trunks or scraping more paint. Best to leave before he was seen and continue connecting the dots without further rocking the boat.

Chapter Thirty-Five

Toss a Coin to Your Gremlins

B y the time Mister Lewis made his way back to the repair shop, the two familiar trenchcoated figures were once more ducking out through the alley.

"Fine," growled the first Gremlin. "We can go to an airport now. Get your itch scratched."

"A big one?" The second Gremlin was practically panting.

"No. You're too excited. Private airfield. Small plane. Less attention in case you get seen."

"Why do you keep acting like I've never done this before?"

"As if you didn't know. Start small. Get your fix. Work your way up to big carriers after I'm confident you've got your nerve back."

The second Gremlin stopped, tilted back his hat and stared daggers in response.

The first Gremlin reached into his coat and produced a large cloth sack that resembled the sort of bag that banks transport money in. He shook it and it jingled with a metallic sound that suggested coins.

"About that," Mister Lewis emerged from the shadows behind them. "We really should have a word about your employment situation. I just keep hearing these stories about contraband metals. You wouldn't happen to know anything about that, would you?"

The first Gremlin dropped the bag, which hit the ground and spilled a few coins of shiny whitish metal onto the ground. He slipped his hand into his coat and produced his gigantic pair of scissors and snipped the air in warning.

"I'm going to go out on a limb and guess those aren't palladium?" Mister Lewis gestured towards the bag.

"What would you know about that?" growled the first Gremlin as the second bent over to secure the spilled coins.

"Palladium's more popular for auto construction than coins, these days. Am I right?"

The first Gremlin thrust his scissors at Mr. Lewis, who sidestepped and swatted at the scissors' handles with his hand. The Gremlin lost his grip, and the scissors flew out of his hands, embedding themselves in a tree.

"You always like to give up this much weight?" Mister Lewis locked his right hand around the Gremlin's bizarrely large nose and lifted him off his feet.

The Gremlin howled.

"And you can keep your hands out where I can see them," Mister Lewis pointed the index finger of his free hand at the second Gremlin with all due menace. "But let's talk about those coins of yours."

The second Gremlin dropped the coin he'd been holding, backed up a step and reached a hand into his coat.

Mister Lewis responded by hurling the first Gremlin into the second. The collision knocked over the second and the two rolled over each other before settling in a pile a few feet further back.

"We both know you saboteurs are no match for a human in a head on fight," said Mister Lewis as he walked over to where the bag of coins lay. "And we also both know your kind is too spongey to suffer lasting injury from my tossing you around, so could we lose the theatrics?"

He leant over the bag and picked up one of the coins that had fallen out.

"Your coins are still warm," he called to the Gremlins. "Fresh out of the oven? We need to talk about what you've been cooking up in this gig of yours."

The first Gremlin rolled back onto his feet and growled.

"You don't know what you're stepping in," whined the second Gremlin.

"That's right, I don't," replied Mister Lewis. "Would you be so good as to enlighten me? Just once, I'd like to do something the easy way."

The first Gremlin grunted in disgust, rolled his eyes and charged Mister Lewis. When he pounced, Mister Lewis caught him by the throat and lifted him up.

"Guys," he continued. "You don't weigh very much. Mass times acceleration doesn't work very well without mass. Physics is working against you. Could we get back to the question? What is it I'm stepping in?"

"Why don't you let me answer that?" The auto repair shop manager appeared at the end of the block behind them. His complexion had changed. The patches of scaly skin were rapidly becoming more pronounced, and the faint green tinge was no longer faint. Of course, the wisps of smoke seeping out his left nostril was a little more disturbing.

Chapter Thirty-Six

Hands On Management

"B y all means," Mister Lewis stepped sideways and backed up, attempting to keep the second Gremlin and The Manager in the same field of vision. He swung the first Gremlin around and held him between himself and The Manager.

"Why don't you think of it as a salvage operation and just walk away?" The Manager's face was now covered in green scales and his hands were starting to change color. Smoke now came out of both nostrils in a steady stream.

"In my experience," replied Mister Lewis, "when someone shifts out of their human form, they usually don't want you to walk away."

The Manager made a noise that was just a little too ugly to be called laughter and stepped forward, progressing from a walk to a jog.

Mister Lewis hurled the first Gremlin at him and started sliding sideways.

The Manager tilted his head back. His jaw dropped further than a human's would and a stream of flame spit out of it. The flame engulfed the first Gremlin, leaving traces of ash to scatter in the wind and burnt itself out roughly where Mister Lewis had been standing when he made the throw.

The Manager charged. Smoke was no longer coming out of his nostrils, but his fingers were changing, with the finger nails growing into thick, bony points.

Mister Lewis greeted him with a kick to the knee. The knee didn't give at all, and it should have.

The Manager swung an emerging claw at him. Mister Lewis ducked the swipe and hit The Manager's groin with a snap kick. The transformation must not have been complete, since this foot connected with something that was still human as The Manager howled in pain and doubled over.

While Mister Lewis contemplated where else might not be armored in scales, he noticed smoke again starting to whisp from The Manager's nostrils. He glanced towards the tree where the first Gremlin's scissors had embedded themselves. No luck. The scissors had faded from existence as the Gremlin was incinerated, which is how it was supposed to work, but that hadn't been the only Gremlin in town.

Mister Lewis grabbed the second Gremlin, who'd started crawling away, by the collar and spun him around. He stuck his hand inside the Gremlin's trench coat. It was a lot like feeling your way around in a closet with the lights turned out, but he eventually seized on the loop of a handle and withdrew a pair of hedge clipper-sized scissors from the coat.

He turned his head to see The Manager starting to move towards an upright position again, smoke now billowing from his nostrils, blacker and with heavier volume than before. More flames were imminent.

He lunged forward with the scissors, opening them and then snapping them shut on The Manager's neck.

He hadn't used a Gremlin's scissors before and was mildly surprised that he felt no resistance as he snipped through the neck. It seemed like a very practical enchantment.

The Manager's severed head fell backwards off the neck and a plume of flame shot straight up into the air.

Mister Lewis exhaled slowly as the body crumpled to the ground.

"I guess The Hippie wasn't wrong about lizard people, after all," he muttered to himself before turning to the surviving Gremlin. "Now, where were we? Oh, that's right. You were going to tell me about the gig. Maybe you should start with the dragon's kid over here?"

Chapter Thirty-Seven

Recycling

"**S**eems you already know a dragon when you see one," squeaked the Gremlin.

"I know the offspring when a dragon mates with a human," growled Mister Lewis. "But let's not get caught up in semantics. Who have you been working for?"

"Nobody, now. You just killed him. And we weren't supposed to be working for him anymore. We just finished our last job."

"That last job was a bagman job, but it was still trafficking in precious metals. How many kinds of metals have you been stealing?"

"I wasn't really counting."

Mister Lewis thrust the point of the scissors under the Gremlin's chin and flashed an insincere smile.

"It was more objects than types of metals," the Gremlin hastily added. "We'd walk over gold from that pawn shop every now and then, but mostly we were taking those things from under the cars."

"Catalytic Converters."

"That's what they called them. And they're really quick to grab. That's what we got paid to do."

"Of course you did. But I know what was being done to the cars in that garage. And I know what they were made of. That's a lot of palladium. How many catalytic converters do you have to steal to get that much metal?"

"Oh, we might not be able to blink and be back home, but we can move freely in a wider radius than you might think. And we've been doing this a long time. Did you really think street gangs were responsible for everything you read in the papers?"

"I think you're exaggerating," said Mister Lewis, "But let's say that's true. Catalytic converters are platinum, palladium and rhodium. The platinum's in that bag of coins, some of it anyway. The palladium's getting smuggled out as car parts. Where's the rhodium going?"

"Not my department, mate. I just did supply runs."

"Fine. And your boss there was melting down the metals and recasting it into coins and car parts?"

"That's a dragon's work, yeah."

"Where's the gold come into it?"

"Not my department, either. But they recycle everything, don't they?"

"Oh," Mister Lewis flashed a facetious grin. "This is an ecologically friendly endeavor, is it?"

"Strewth! No wasting paper and ink marking up bank notes. We just traffic in honest metals. The traditional ways are the best!"

"So, you made coins with the gold, too?"

"I never said that," the Gremlin's eyes shifted around and refused to stay still.

"Sure, you didn't. Can't say that I've ever heard of rhodium coins before, though?"

Now the Gremlin's facial expression was genuine confusion, followed by a shrug.

"Fine," Mister Lewis continued. "What can you tell me about the person who drove that fake Gremlin out of the garage?"

"Wasn't a regular," said the Gremlin. "I did think the car was a nice tribute, though."

"Utterly touching. So that's it? You were just walking away?"

"Not walking away. Going home. We were never supposed to be over here this long. They were winding this thing down anyway."

"And you just want to go home, now?"

"That's right. Not like I could go back to procuring those converters if my boss is dead. I could just be on my way."

"To an airport?"

"Yeah, like I was saying, I can't just blink myself home or I would have a long time ago."

"There's a problem with that."

"And what's the problem?"

"I know what you were going to do at the airport to start getting your nerve back."

The Gremlin was silent.

Mister Lewis opened the scissors and snipped off the Gremlin's head. As the head hit the ground, both the Gremlin's head and body blinked out of reality. At the same time, the scissors faded away leaving him holding nothing. It was the easiest way to clean up that part of the mess.

He stepped over to the remains of The Manager. The flames had stopped spitting from the neck and had self-cauterized the wound. He placed the head on the manager's stomach, then gathered up the stray platinum coins, placed them back in the sack, put the sack next to the head and started dragging the body back to the repair shop.

Chapter Thirty-Eight

When He Got There, the Cupboard was Bare

M ister Lewis found the auto repair shop deserted and the alley door unlocked, which was convenient enough. One does not like to linger in plain view long enough to pick a lock while dragging the mutilated and no longer human corpse of a building's owner.

Upon entering, he dropped the corpse and headed straight to the storeroom in the back, where he'd spotted the catalytic converters on his last visit. The room had been cleaned out.

He went back to the shop's main room. Up against the wall was a curious collection of equipment. Graphite molds of various sizes. Scissor tongs that also came in different sizes. A large steel chamber lined with bricks that could only be some kind of kiln.

There wasn't a heating source for the kiln, but that was probably The Manager's smoldering breath. And, really, that was a stealthier way to handle it. If they'd attracted enough attention for somebody to audit the place, there'd be no questions about why so many heating supplies, say propane, had been purchased or what they were being used for. Slick and quiet.

Examining it, the kiln was clean. Spotless, really. The molds, not so much. The larger molds, which looked to be for auto parts, had traces of what was likely palladium around the edges. The smaller molds looked to be coins and had bits of gold flecked here and there. He couldn't find any coin molds with traces of platinum around them, so either that wasn't the final batch or it was done elsewhere.

He opened the bag of coins he'd confiscated from the Gremlins. The coins all seemed to be of the same shape and casting. They also didn't fit any of the coin molds lying around. Perhaps the catalytic converters weren't the only things that had been cleared out. He pulled out his cell phone and took pictures of the molds. What kind of coins were being made could be sorted out later.

Further inspection of the room found a dumpster in the back that was half-filled with what was likely the crushed remains of more graphite molds. A dragon's offspring would be strong enough to do that and it was more evidence that someone was closing up shop in this location.

The paperwork was missing from the front, but that was OK. He already knew The Billionaire owned the place, had been on premises and took possession of an altered vehicle. And it wasn't like the police would have any idea what to make of a half-dragon running a theft ring with gremlins.

He placed The Manager's body and head in the kiln, then located the garage's supply of brake fluid. He marinated the body with brake fluid and left a nice pool of it in the bottom of the kiln. Then he fashioned a torch from some rags and a piece of wood broken off a crate. The torch was lit and tossed in the kiln. It made a satisfying noise as the rest of the flames sprang to life.

What was left should suitably confuse whoever found it, assuming they weren't part of the scheme. They'd probably think the bones were some kind of prank.

Chapter Thirty-Nine
All Sales Are Final

T he storm still raged outside the podcasting studio.
"That's navel-gazing at its finest," mused The Swede in an earnest deadpan.

"Excuse me for being a hygiene proponent," moaned The Hippie. "Lint is a breeding ground for bacteria, weird odors and I bet it's probably flammable. Do you want your belly button going up in flames?"

"I find it unlikely my navel will spontaneously combust."

"Oh, fine. Rip on me for unsound judgement, but the second I do something responsible with my body, do I get any positive reinforcement?"

"What was the topic of this podcast again?"

"Apparently," moaned The Hippie, "changing the topic is our subject today. So, fine, I'll change the topic. Why don't we talk about our reptilian overlords?"

"Are they keeping you down?" asked The Swede, dry as ever.

"They're keeping everyone down. It's a class war. It's a fiscal war."

"It's a metaphor."

"You just keep on thinking that. But what if it's not just the man keeping us down?"

"Are you referring to your impulsive adventures in digital investing? To your investment in Schatzhorde des Drachen? Do you think the dragon the crypto coin is named after is a lizard that is keeping you down?"

"Reptiles is as reptiles do," proclaimed The Hippie.

"And do you have an update on this glorious investment?" asked The Swede.

"The update is the investors keep disappearing."

"You seem to still be with us."

"And how do you explain our last few podcasts?"

The Swede paused and frowned. Things that were very useful to a podcast audience.

"I think you are more valuable to our podcast network than a phantasmal force that wants to steal your coins," The Swede was perhaps a bit less dry than usual. "But the weather is the weather."

"Coincidence?"

"Happenstance."

"And the fact that I cannot sell my coins?"

"What is that delightful phrase the children in the crypto field like to use? 'Do your research?' Did you do your research before investing?"

"Oh, I'm doing my research all right," The Hippie's eyes widened and glazed over. "I wasn't the first soldier to fall, but if my investment sinks, I'm going down with the ship."

"Perhaps our podcast is about tortured metaphors?" interjected The Swede.

"I know where the owner of the Schatzhorde des Drachen platform is going to be today and I'm going to get answers for myself."

"Would you consider a restraining order to be a kind of answer? That is an answer you might be able to get."

"Are you making light of ten missing persons cases?"

"I'm making light of your determination to test the limits of what our network's lawyers can extricate you from. Please have the consideration to keep me excluded from any defamation suits that follow from your adventures."

"We'll see if you're still smiling tomorrow. We'll see if I'm even here to see if you're still smiling."

"Listeners," sighed The Swede. "In case you were wondering, we will not be having a remote broadcast tomorrow."

The Hippie stormed out of the studio.

Chapter Forty

Executive Orders

"**P**arts of the case are making more sense," Mister Lewis sat before The Head of HR. "I still can't tell you where cryptocurrencies fit into this scheme, but The Billionaire appears to be part of an overly complicated scheme to steal and smuggle palladium to Guatemala. Although, that almost makes more sense than a legitimate mine popping up out of nowhere down there."

"Are you saying the mine is a laundering operation?" asked The Head of HR.

"Sure seems like it. And an expensive one, too. Then again, the idea of doing that is so preposterous, nobody would think to question it. The big picture is even stranger than that. I can now link The Billionaire directly to supernatural activity. Gremlins were being employed to steal the catalytic convertors the palladium was coming from."

"Enough to supply a mine?"

"I did say preposterous. It's possible there were other sources, but the Gremlins appear to have been stealing a high volume and it isn't clear how wide a geography they were operating in. The catalytic converter theft could just be a small facet of a wider scheme. Based on what I saw being loaded onto that boat, they're dealing in tons and I can't be sure where it's all coming from. That's tangential to my assignment, though. The important thing is that we now have a concrete link between The Billionaire and the supernatural goings on your people have been wondering about."

"And this link to the supernatural would be using Gremlins as thieves?" The Head of HR frowned.

"I'd probably call them procurement agents, given the scope, but that's not the big reveal. It turns out the manager of that auto repair shop wasn't human."

"Oh?"

"Well, half-human. The other half was dragon. A crossbreed."

"You mean like a mule that breathes fire?"

"That's a simplification, but close enough."

"And it explains the... cremation of witnesses you've been running into."

"Not only explains," Mister Lewis nodded. "One of those Gremlins was reduced to ash in front of my eyes. Also seems likely that The Manager's breath was used to melt the various metals before recasting them for easier smuggling."

"If it's similar to a mule, does that mean it's a male dragon and female human?"

"You'll sleep better if you don't know the mechanics of it."

"But that's the end of it? You've eliminated the muscle?"

"Let me back up a little," Mister Lewis said after a lengthy exhale. "This is a lot of things, but straight-forward isn't one of them. You remember that exporter I ran down after the initial assassination attempt?"

"The first one to get cremated?"

"Yes. That exporter had pretty much the same skin condition as The Manager at the auto shop."

"Another half... are you saying one sibling killed the other?"

"That's the working theory."

"And... what? You think there could be more of them?"

"It certainly seems possible. Look, if you have enough money to throw around, there's muscle to be had. We've also two succubi on the payroll and somebody produced some Slugs of Lyssa. And I didn't tell you about my last two stops before I had to decapitate that Manager."

"This is going to be bad, isn't it?"

"It could be worse," Mister Lewis shrugged. "First off, I ran into that Manager at what turned out to be a fake recycling shop."

"Fake how?"

"Fake two ways. They sort of were recycling. Stripping off gold and platinum and rhodium – the pricier stuff, but leaving all the things like copper that normally get recycled. Near as I can tell, that was just extra scraps for the smuggling and whatever else they're doing with precious metals. But before that, they were restoring any hard drives that came their way and stealing any financial information that was on them."

"You mean you've finally got a crime tied directly to..."

"No. The Manager was the cut out and I burned the place down. As you were saying, that could take too long. We might not have a ton of time. They're not going to be operating out of that place anymore, though. And then there was the latest stock short."

"We saw something that looked like it was aborted?" The Head of HR said.

"Yeah, I got a sort of friend of a friend phone call and managed to get between the company and the scam. And that's the bad news. The Billionaire has some sort of non-human sorcerer on the payroll. A couple employees had been incinerated in the alley and replaced by Changelings."

"Elves?"

"No, the other kind. Enchanted logs. But it's Fae magic and humans can't perform Fae magic, so we've got another problem floating around."

"And you think the incineration of the employees was done by the now-beheaded Manager?"

"I really wish I knew," Mister Lewis shook his head. "The Billionaire seems to have a deep bench."

"So," began The Head of HR, "Hypothetically speaking, we could have a werewolf crash into the recording studio next?"

"In theory, yes. It's always possible to restaff a vacancy. And the longer this goes on, the greater the chances it happens."

"In that case, I might have some good news. When you obstructed that last short, the holding company behind it ceased doing business."

"What exactly do you mean by that?"

"It appears to have had its assets transferred out of it and looks to be inactive. It's a little early to tell, but that's happened to multiple holding companies thought to be controlled by The Billionaire."

"Maybe I spooked somebody with the fire and short going south, back-to-back?"

"Some of the businesses have the appearance of being rolled up."

"And it looked like they had cleaned out the garage and were abandoning the building, too."

"The Billionaire is a very private person. Avoiding attention would be in character. If The Billionaire thought the spotlight was coming, and from what you say, there might be a reason for that... this could be scrubbing the operations and walking away. Do you think this could be over?"

"That would depend on what needed scrubbing. Is that cryptocurrency operation winding down?"

"If so, it hasn't started, but that doesn't mean it's not going to."

"A lot of people are going to scream if that coin just goes offline. Look at what happened to FTX. And the people who've been close enough to linking The Billionaire to it and went nosing around have been turning to ash. The first question is whether that scam is winding down and the second question is whether your podcasters are a loose end that needs tidying up."

"And until we know which way that goes..."

"Then we don't know, as you put it, if a werewolf is going to crash into the recording studio. It might be over, or it might be about to get very dangerous."

"That sounds expensive."

"Hard to say. Even if everything is just being walked away from, the possibility for more reprisals exists. If The Billionaire lays the blame for all this unravelling at their feet, that might mean something will come for them after everyone has disappeared. These things sometimes move at their own pace."

"And such things are beyond our control," The Head of HR sighed. "Oh, well. We have an obligation to protect our employees and at least we have a better idea what we're dealing with. Do we have any idea what the end game is?"

"About half of the operations seem to be about winding up with clean money. The palladium is getting laundered through a mine. Shorting a stock is just shorting a stock. But the whole cryptocurrency business that started your involvement? That's something else, as is whatever they're doing with the stolen financial and identity information. If that's being laundered, I haven't run into it yet. Some of the stolen platinum is being used to pay under the table expenses, but I have no idea what's being done with the rhodium from the catalytic converters. The gold being recast as coins? That's clear out of left field."

"It's funny you should mention rhodium," said The Head of HR. "We do have some information that The Billionaire has been buying up a lot of rhodium. It's possible the rhodium is being hoarded, not sold."

"Where's it being delivered?"

"One of The Billionaire's suspected holding companies owns a building in the financial district. We suspect there's some kind of a vault in the basement. And let me check... no, that one doesn't appear to have disappeared from the records yet."

"Right" Mister Lewis snorted. "This whole thing does give off an underground lair vibe, doesn't it? Is there any activity around gold in those records you've been digging up?"

"Not bullion. But... you remember there was a coin collector's shop on the list of direct holdings?"

"As in coin molds being found at the garage?"

"Right, well, supposedly The Billionaire is going to be at some sort of rare coin auction at the shop, today. Our understanding is that one of the lots up for bid are from The Billionaire's personal collection."

"And I suppose it would be too convenient if these were gold coins being sold?"

"I couldn't tell you that. It came up through The Hippie's backchannels. I believe The Hippie was planning on being at the auction."

"That sounds like an amazingly bad idea," Mister Lewis was halfway to the door as he spoke. "If there's any more mystical help on the payroll and The Hippie forces a confrontation..."

Chapter Forty-One

I'll See Your Bid and Raise You a Body

T he auction hadn't quite started when Mister Lewis arrived at the coin shop. There was a moderately sized crowd milling about and viewing the coins up for sale. A quick query indicated which lot belonged to The Billionaire and it was an unusual one: a lot of 20 Caligula aurei coins.

An aureus coin was a gold coin of Roman vintage, which could be exchanged for 25 of the more common silver denarii coins back in the day. The Caligula version of the aureus was only struck for a handful of years and very few were thought to still exist. Convenient that 20 should just appear in one place and that five of them looked new to the world... or "mint," as the collectors would refer to them.

Mister Lewis scanned the room. The Hippie didn't seem to be here... yet. Nor was The Billionaire anywhere to be seen. He doubted his luck was good enough that neither would show and decided to pass the time with a closer examination of the coins. He scanned the room a second time, looking for bodyguards or enforcers. If The Billionaire had "special" help in the room, they were doing a good job of concealing their true nature.

First, he pulled out his phone, pulled up the photo he'd taken of the coin mold and zoomed in. Sure enough, the lettering around the edge of the coin matched up with the mold. He couldn't be sure that the face of Caligula in the center of the coin matched up exactly, just by glancing at it, but it was close enough not to leave him with an excessive amount of doubts.

Looking at the coins, five of them did indeed look brand new. The description of the lot noted how rare a mint condition Caligula aureus was and that prior to this collection going up for auction, less than five were thought to exist, much less five available at the same time. That wasn't the least bit suspicious.

Of the remaining fifteen, three looked like something very heavy had been dropped on them and twelve had varying degrees of scratches. Scratches that looked more than a little bit like claw or talon marks, although he didn't figure a numismatic room would recognize them as that.

Glancing around the room again, he still wasn't seeing The Hippie or The Billionaire and he really needed to get eyes on at least one of them. He did notice The Auctioneer milling about, though. That was something he could work with in the meantime.

"Have these aurei been authenticated?" he asked while beckoning The Auctioneer over.

"Of course," replied The Auctioneer. "While we can't be sure of the exact date, our suspicion is these would be from later in the production cycle. Perhaps from 40 or 41AD."

Seeing a plausible excuse to use his monocle, Mister Lewis nonchalantly reached into his pocket and held it over a coin in a theatrical fashion.

"I can't help but notice there's no patina on these coins," said Mister Lewis.

"Gold does clean up a bit easier than silver."

"That's fair," agreed Mister Lewis as he looked up and brought the monocle with him to better scan the room. The first thing he noticed was The Auctioneer's new look: it was another animated log with sticks for arms. "But how do you account for the natural variation in the coins?"

"I'm not sure I follow."

"Just look at them. The size is exactly the same on each of them."

Mister Lewis moved his head back and forth in mock dismay, waving the monocle as he did so and scanning the room. The Auctioneer was the only thing out of place, but that probably meant more trouble was either better disguised or lurking nearby.

"These coins were found together," replied The Auctioneer. "It's reasonable to assume they were made from the same die."

"I'm not sure I'd go that far. Look at the depth of the features on those heads. Identical. You just don't get that when they're striking one coin at a time."

He'd been speaking just loud enough, the prospective bidders were starting to come over for a look.

"Correct me if I'm wrong," continued Mister Lewis, "but Caligula aurei were supposed to be struck, not cast? These look like they were cast from a mold."

The crowd murmured in general agreement.

"Where did you say these coins came from?" asked Mister Lewis.

The auctioneer wasn't speaking and was apparently at a loss for a diplomatic response.

"They came from the ground," a booming voice emanated from the back of the room as The Billionaire finally appeared. "Mother Earth often does an excellent job of protecting precious things from the ravages of time."

"I've been known to find shiny things in even more surprising places," Mister Lewis flashed a smile that spoke of mischief. If his client wasn't yet here, perhaps he could make enough of a scene to clear the room before The Hippie arrived? "It's really amazing what turns up in my garage, for instance."

The Billionaire's nostrils flared and a noise that was half snort and half growl emerged as The Billionaire took a deep breath and exhaled.

"And sometimes you lose things in a garage," The Billionaire stepped closer.

That was when The Hippie finally showed up.

"But that's not where the real coin action is," The Hippie sauntered over, radiating a cocktail of moral indignation and irrational confidence. "Not if you're looking for a real appreciation of value."

The Billionaire's head tilted, mouth twisting first into a frown, then a smile, then something undefinable that showed teeth.

"You are a different sort of collector, then?" The Billionaire's head tilted the other way now, looking The Hippie up and down. "Did you turn on, tune in and drop out of traditional currency?"

"You could say I'm into alternate forms of currency," The Hippie replied with narrowing eyes.

The Billionaire snorted again. There was something about the way The Billionaire's nostrils were flaring that put Mister Lewis on edge.

"Perhaps we should leave," Mister Lewis flashed The Hippie a hard look.

"No," said The Hippie, voice rising half an octave. "Let's discuss digital coins. Everyone knows that's where the action is."

"We don't have that kind of coin here," said The Auctioneer, trying to diffuse the situation.

The Billionaire's eyes flickered towards The Hippie and then to Mister Lewis.

"Ahhh," hissed The Billionaire. "I was wondering who you were. You're the one who's been following me, aren't you?"

Before Mister Lewis could reply, The Hippie strode over and stuck a finger into The Billionaire's shoulder.

"I've got a bone to pick with you," screamed The Hippie. "You're not fooling anybody. I know exactly what you are."

"This is not the time," began Mister Lewis, pulling The Hippie by the arm.

"No," hissed The Billionaire, a little louder this time. "I want to hear this. What am I? Invoke the power of my true name."

Mister Lewis, fearing what was about to come, stepped in front of The Hippie.

"A thief is what you are," The Hippie's head popped over the shoulder of Mister Lewis. "You stole my coins from Schatzhorde des Drachen – The Dragon's Treasure Hoard. You stole coins from Schatzhorde des Drachen. We can't sell them because they don't exist anymore. Thief!"

"And your true name is Fool," The Billionaire's eyes rolled. "Only a fool thinks anyone but a dragon can own a dragon's coins. What do you know about hoards?"

Mister Lewis mouthed an expletive.

"I was almost done with this identity anyway," The Billionaire sighed. "I suppose there's no point in dragging it out any longer. I'll just have to move the hoard a little quicker than planned. You know what I am? Step up and claim your prize."

The Billionaire began to grow and not proportionally. In a half second, The Billionaire was both two feet taller and a foot wider. The Billionaire's skin shifted to a patchy green, then to scales.

Mister Lewis dove to the floor taking The Hippie with him.

The Billionaire's body was no longer human. The clothes tore away as wings sprouted from the back. There was no head visible, as The Billionaire's head was through the ceiling. There were, however, plenty of pieces of the ceiling falling to the floor, along with dust and assorted rubble.

When the dust cleared, Mister Lewis looked up. A two-story tall dragon, in all its emerald glory was flexing its wings. And it was just as well it was flexing those wings. Those wings had been shielding much of the room from a partial building collapse. The outer wall was gone, and the room now opened up onto the street.

"Excuse me while I clear the room," The Dragon's voice was like a steam leak echoing in a barrel. The

Dragon opened its mouth and spat flame in a wide arc, careful to aim over the heads of Mister Lewis, The Hippie and The Auctioneer, but reducing everything else to char and ash. "Now, where was I? Oh, yes. The fool wants to see my treasure hoard? After all the trouble you've gone to, it would be rude of me not to accommodate you. Afterwards, I can make you a snack. Are you crunchy, fool?"

The Auctioneer reached out for The Hippie.

"Get lost, you ambulatory twig," Mister Lewis shoved The Auctioneer, who tumbled backwards into the burning rumble.

It only took a moment for The Auctioneer's arm to catch fire. The flame ran up the arm, and as it reached the torso, the illusion of human life flickered away and the log at the center of the Changeling lay still and burning.

"That's not how I like to get wood," squeaked The Hippie.

"We need to go," said Mister Lewis.

"And you see through Changelings," The Dragon's voice boomed. "That does explain a detail or two. Do you also share my affinity for fire? Does the state of this room remind you of another building you recently left? I wonder if it does?"

"And I suppose you animated those Changelings, yourself?" Mister Lewis half-glanced over his shoulder towards The Dragon.

"They're much more obedient than the living ones. Oh, you mean the magic. Yes, my kind is more adept with that than humans are. Fae magic holds no secrets to one such as myself. I can see I must give out two rewards this day. Both of you, face me and reap the fruits of your labors."

Mister Lewis turned to face The Dragon. He opened his mouth, but before a word could emerge, one of The Dragon's wings slapped him off his feet and clear into the street. Then the wings flapped and The Dragon left the ground. The Dragon extended a clawed foot and closed it around The Hippie, who was too terrified to speak or move.

"You're wet," said The Dragon with mild disgust. "That's alright. You'll be dry enough before the snack. I'll take care of that myself."

The Dragon's wings flapped harder, gaining altitude... and the wind they kicked up caused the building to finish its collapse.

"I think I shall enjoy reading about the city inspectors rationalizing what happened to my coin shop," The Dragon giggled, before flying north.

Mister Lewis emerged from the cloud of dust kicked up by the secondary collapse and watched The Dragon disappear behind the buildings in the skyline.

"That Hippie is a poor excuse for a princess," he muttered to himself. "And I've never been mistaken for Saint George."

Chapter Forty-Two

Return to Sender

"**D**o you have the address handy for that holding company The Billionaire was having Rhodium sent to?" Mister Lewis said into his phone.

The Head of HR did, but wanted to know why.

"Turns out The Billionaire is a dragon."

"Are you speaking metaphorically?" asked The Head of HR.

"Nope. Green scales, wings, the whole nine yards. Some dragons can take human form. This one shifted back to dragon form, grabbed The Hippie in a claw and flew off."

"I thought you said The Billionaire checked out as human when you staked out the eSports operation."

"No, I said there weren't any illusions. When a dragon changes form, that's a physical transformation. The human form, itself, is real."

"Fine. Then what are The Bill... er, this dragon's intentions with my employee?"

"It sounded like there was going to be a barbeque."

"Can you retrieve my employee?"

"It depends on how fast I can locate them. The Dragon said something about packing it up, so it's likely they're headed towards the dragon's lair. The Dragon is probably assuming it would take someone a few days to untangle the paper trail from The Billionaire's public holdings to wherever they are, so if that address the rhodium has been sent to is the lair, I didn't get the impression anyone was done packing it up and they'll probably still be there. If The Dragon gets hungry, though... we'll see."

"This is going to cost extra, isn't it?"

"The cost goes down if I don't survive the attempt," Mister Lewis closed his phone and looked for a cab.

Chapter Forty-Three
The Honored Guest

"This is the weirdest dungeon I've ever been in," grumbled The Hippie, looking around at the cavern-like space they sat in. If it were empty, you might think it was a warehouse, except warehouses tend not to be in sub-sub-basements, nor are they typically several feet deep in precious metals.

"No, I'm afraid I have neither whip, nor riding crop," replied The Dragon. "It also isn't a dungeon, you peasant. It is a lair. Did you not want to see what a real treasure hoard looks like before you die?"

The Hippie looked to both sides and frowned.

"OK, I get the whole Scrooge McDuck thing with mountains of coins to swim in. But these aren't gold coins. They're silver. That's kind of, you know, cheap for a lair, isn't it?"

"You think this is common?" The Dragon reared up, nostrils starting to smoke. "You're too ignorant to know what you're looking at. That's not silver, that's rhodium. A far rarer metal than gold. Please, I must have some standards."

"They make coins out of that?" The Hippie picked up coin and stared at it in puzzlement.

"Mostly, I melt it down and cast my own coins. It's traditional to have a portion of your hoard in coins and one makes due with the resources at hand."

"Then why did you put Queen Elizabeth on your coins?" The Hippie held the coin up. "You don't sound British."

"That coin is a South Sea Dragon. It is legal tender for 100 Tuvaluan dollars."

"You made that up."

"Were you even educated as a child? Tuvalu is an island in the South Pacific, near what your people would call Samoa and Tonga."

"If it's near Samoa and Tonga, how come I've never heard of any professional wrestlers from there?"

The Dragon crouched down, getting eye to eye with The Hippie, who coughed from the smoke seeping from The Dragon's nostrils.

"What's the matter?" asked The Dragon. "My smoke isn't the kind you're used to? Now pay attention! I have, at considerable expense, acquired a selection of Tuvaluan Sea Dragon coins because authenticity is also a tradition and it's good to have somewhere your coin will spend with minimal fuss. If you select another coin from the pile beneath your unlearned feet, you will find most of the coins are larger. A Tuvaluan Sea Dragon is one ounce. I cast my own coins at a weight of three ounces. These are not the copper and nickel fare you keep in your pocket. Show some respect for what you hold in your hand!"

"Seems a little too fancy to do laundry with," observed The Hippie. "What else do people use coins for these days? I'm categorically against conspicuous consumption."

The Dragon, neglecting to consider the source, howled in frustration.

Chapter Forty-Four

The Moving Party

M ister Lewis appraised the building from across the street. The address the rhodium had been shipped to was a relatively new looking mid-rise office building. Nothing particularly interesting about it, but you wouldn't expect a dragon to be flamboyant about the entrance to its lair, if that's what this was. The only thing interesting about it was the kind of deliveries that were being received.

With that in mind, he circled the building and found a loading dock with four semi-trailers backed up to it. Four people, obviously the truck drivers, were huddled by the edge of the dock.

"I'm with the union," Mister Lewis lied. "You boys being treated alright?"

"The usual," the first truck driver shrugged. "Something wrong?"

"Probably not," replied Mister Lewis. "But we heard about something we wanted to check on. Wouldn't want anyone pulling a fast one on you. You all going to the same place?"

"Yeah," said the second driver. "The guy in charge of the dock said something about Florida. Supposed to be a castle. We all figure it's Disney stuff, but he's not giving us the full address until we ship out."

"Who else would build a castle?" Mister Lewis deadpanned. "How long they had you waiting?"

"Eh, we just got here," said the third driver. "Just got the call. Whatever they're moving, they're in a big hurry and its last minute."

"That checks out," Mister Lewis replied solemnly. "You get a manifest for what you're carrying?"

The truck drivers nodded that they hadn't.

"Who's in charge of receiving for these clowns?"

The first truck driver gestured towards the end of the loading dock.

The loading dock door opened into a hallway. Five steps in was an office where a man with his back to the door stood over a burning trashcan, slowly feeding the fire from a handful of papers.

Mister Lewis quietly entered the room, grabbed the man by the back of his neck and bounced his head off the nearest desk. Then he closed the door and examined the scattered papers that had been in his hand. They were receiving slips for shipments of rhodium, mostly bullion.

Someone was cleaning up ahead of the move. He wondered if the truck drivers were likely to be eaten when they arrived at that castle?

The desk revealed shipping manifests headed towards a "Nexus Castle" at an address the Mister Lewis thought might be physically inside the Everglades. There were too many suspicious documents in the room to leave much doubt this was the right place. It didn't necessarily mean the entire staff knew about the true nature of their boss, though it suggested enough of them knew not everything was on the up and up. No need to be gentle if he wasn't dealing with angels. And it left the question of where exactly The Dragon was holed up?

He locked the man in the office's closet, figuring if he was still in the building when the guy woke up, he was already screwed. Before he did, he removed a swipe card with the building's name printed on it from the man's belt and clipped it on the front of his jacket. He also swiped a can of disinfectant spray, since he had already made the acquaintance of The Dragon's executive staff.

Then he went looking for a stairwell.

Chapter Forty-Five

Efficiency Vs. Pillaging

"There may be no point to educating you," lamented The Dragon. "Perhaps, I should just eat you and be done with it?"

"Why don't you educate me on where my Schatzhorde des Drachen crypto coins are?" The Hippie's contempt won out over terror.

"Still on about that?" The Dragon's eyes rolled. "Very well. Let us come full circle. Your lamentations and threats started your journey. They can end them, as well. There are no Schatzhorde des Drachen coins."

"That's impossible! I paid good money for those coins! I want them back so I can sell them for market value."

"What is wrong with you?" asked The Dragon in exasperation. "You never had them in the first place. You had an email receipt and access to a website with a screen that showed your purchases. Did you ever see Schatzhorde des Drachen listed on an exchange? No. Did you ever have the opportunity to make a transaction with it? No. I suppose you called it an altcoin?"

"Of course, it's an altcoin! What else would it be?"

"The more realistic among your kind would call it a shitcoin. That's at least as common a term as altcoin. They, too, would be wrong. As I said before, Schatzhorde des Drachen did not exist."

"Then how did its value keep going up?"

"Because I said it was going up. I suppose you think I honored the statement of maximum coins available, too? Ha! I oversold three times over. I could have called it a Bialystock & Bloom coin, but that would be too on the nose. Don't worry about losing your life's savings. I won't let you starve. Nor will I let myself starve."

"And you had that island put the Queen on your coin because she's a lizard person, like you?"

"What?" stammered The Dragon. "No. It's a former colony of hers and I'm not what you'd call a person. You don't actually believe that old lizard person rumor, do you?"

The Hippie stared back in a cold rage.

"I see," said The Dragon. "I've never met someone who actually believed that before. Is there something wrong with your brain? Something actually physically wrong with it? Perhaps a disease? Are you contagious or would that go away with a proper roasting? I would hate to contract such a disease from eating you."

"And all this?" asked The Hippie. "Why are you bothering scamming people with promises of happy financial returns when you're sitting on a pile of... whatever this is..."

"Rhodium," corrected The Dragon. "It is called rhodium. Very well, I shall try to explain, but I fear the terms may not be simple enough for you. In the first place, to quote your species' great philosopher, W.C. Fields, 'You can't cheat an honest man.' There is great amusement in seeing what special creatures leap at the chance to level up their wealth so quickly.

"And in the second place, I shall break with the philosophies of Fields and attempt to, in his vernacular, 'smarten up a chump.' Yes, I can simply swoop down from the sky and take what I want. That's a very slow way to accumulate treasure, though. In the case of a truly rare metal, there's only so much of it in one place. And if there were a sizeable amount, there's the matter of transporting it. It's much more efficient to acquire native currency and use it to have the treasure sent to me."

"You mean," stammered The Hippie. "You mean I'm the victim of a virtual pillaging?"

"At last," cried The Dragon. "A vision of truth dances before your eyes. There are so many ways to pillage fools in this brave, new world. All one has to do is disappear before the fools discover what has happened and assemble their torches. Then you establish a new human identity in another place and start anew. Who knows, maybe I shall pillage some of them a second time?"

The Hippie stood slack jawed for a moment before sitting down in a fog of cognitive dissonance on a pile of coins.

"Try not to drool on yourself," sighed The Dragon. "I need to start packing. We can continue this discussion and establish if you're safe to eat when I've finished."

The Dragon moved over to the wall, lifted a panel and pulled out a four-foot-wide hose. After leaving the hose on top a large pile of coins, The Dragon returned to the wall, hit a button and the sound of a gigantic vacuum cleaner filled the room as the hose started sucking up coins.

"What are you doing?" shouted The Hippie over the noise.

"Packing," growled The Dragon. "This is the most efficient way to collect coins."

"Everybody knows vacuuming coins will break the vacuum," The Hippie cried with an increasingly vacant look.

"Do you think I can't afford to get something more durable built?" The Dragon yelled back over the din. "Fine, perhaps I'll show you."

The Dragon returned to the wall and turned off the vacuum.

"For one to truly enjoy their hoard," continued The Dragon. "It is customary for one to bathe in their treasures."

The Hippie attempted to speak.

"Yes, like your precious Scrooge McDuck," The Dragon cut off the interruption. "But I am an innovator. While it currently is convenient to move the hoard by this means for easier packaging before its eventual transport, that was not the original purpose of this device. Oh, no. This is a pleasure system."

The Dragon pointed a claw towards an inset circle of metal in the ceiling and the large chain hanging next to it that appeared to originate from the floor above.

"The coins are suctioned up through that hose into a reservoir on the floor above. When I pull that chain, the portal opens and the reservoir falls through, letting me bathe in my rhodium hoard."

"Was that designed when you were hoarding gold?" asked The Hippie.

"Why?" The Dragon's eyes narrowed to slits.

"Because then you'd be into golden showers," The Hippie laughed hysterically.

"Yes," smoke was again leaving The Dragon's nostrils. "There definitely is something wrong with your brain. I won't eat contaminated meat. Instead, let us give you a final education. I shall take a shower, as you so commonly put it, so you make observe its grandeur. Then I shall place you under the portal and you shall also take a shower and we'll see if a ton of rhodium leaves an impression upon you."

The Dragon reached for the chain and tugged.

Chapter Forty-Six

Caverns of the Urban Dungeon

T he swipe card worked like a charm. The building was in a chaotic state of frenzy, but when the employees noticed the swipe card, they paid Mister Lewis no mind and went back to their tasks... which largely seemed to be shouting about crates, which no one seemed to know the location of.

The people who seemed the most exasperated appeared to be coming from the elevator and exiting while it was on the way up. This seemed consistent with The Head of HR's suspicions of a basement vault. Not really wanting to have a conversation with anyone, he took the stairwell down as far as it would go.

When he exited the bottom of the stairs, there was less chaos in the corridor. There was what appeared to be some kind of guard at a very large door at the end of the hall from the elevator. Every so often, the elevator would arrive and one or two people would walk over, wanting to get through the door. They would be none too gently rebuffed and told nobody was getting in until they had proper shipping crates with them and then The Guard – and only The Guard – would make sure those crates were properly sealed.

It seemed there was a trust deficit going around and that sure seemed like a good sign for finding a secret vault.

Mister Lewis lingered in the stairwell long enough to produce his monocle and have a glance at the guard. Sure enough, it wasn't human. On the other hand, it was a slightly larger log than the ones he'd previously encountered. The sticks that made up its limbs were much thicker. Did that mean it was better suited for combat?

"We've got a problem with the crates," Mister Lewis popped out of the stairwell and jogged over to The Guard, feigning being out of breath.

"Now, what?" barked The Guard, who had clearly been hearing a lot of excuses.

A cigarette lighter appeared in the left hand of Mister Lewis.

The guard took a reflexive step backwards and bumped into the door.

The can of disinfectant spray appeared in his right hand. The lighter lit and so did a burst of the spray. The improvised flamethrower's fruit struck the guard squarely in the chest.

The guard's hand flew up, its face contorted, and then a second burst of flame finished igniting the log at its center. The illusion of the guard disappeared and the Changeling collapsed in a pile of burning wood and made an oddly metallic clanging noise.

Now that he could get a better look at it, this was actually some kind of vault door. Possibly an antique. It looked like it was probably thick and the key hole on the lock was immense. Naturally, the door was locked.

He looked down at the pile of burning wood. That clanging noise had apparently been a large metal key the Changeling must have been carrying. He stomped out the flames and used a handkerchief as makeshift oven mitt to pick it up. It fit in the lock. It was probably another reason to have such a large Changeling on the door, because that key did not turn easily. Eventually it did and the door creaked open.

He looked back towards the elevator. It wasn't heading back down... yet. He kicked the pieces of wood inside the door and relocked it. Then he arranged the wood into a pile and re-lit it. It was hard to be too careful when your back was potentially exposed.

What he found when he turned around to survey the room was unusual, to say the least. The door had opened onto a wide landing above another set of stairs. He took two steps down a stairway, just far enough to duck his head to see what was below, and discovered that the next level seemed to go the length of the building. A large and odd-looking machine loomed over what could only be described as an enormous, building-length dumpster. And the dumpster was partially filled with platinum coins.

No. Not platinum. This was where the rhodium was being delivered, alright. It didn't seem like rhodium now being in the form of coins should be a great shock.

The machine then sprang to life, sounding a little too much like an airplane engine and a spout above it started spitting more coins into the dumpster. After a bit, it stopped.

He took a few steps down the stairs, only to freeze in place as the back end of the dumpster raised up and the coins started to pour out the front of it.

Chapter Forty-Seven

Killer Showers are Expensive

T he Dragon yanked hard on the chain. The metal disc in the ceiling slid back and rhodium coins rained down from the opening, bouncing off the head, wings and upper torso of The Dragon before crashing to the floor. It sounded like a thousand cups full of coins were being shaken at once.

After 30 seconds, The Dragon tugged on the chain again and the shower stopped.

"There," said The Dragon. "Was that not a glorious sight? A life changing sight? Few know such luxury."

"Doesn't that hurt?" whined The Hippie, tenderly rubbing a welt caused by a stray coin that bounced wide.

"Didn't you know? Dragons have thick skins. Do you have thick skin, my crypto-opportunist friend? Why don't we find out what happens when you get showered with good fortune?"

The Dragon plucked The Hippie off the pile of coins with two talons.

"This is the wrong kind of stoned, man," yelped The Hippie.

The Hippie was then placed directly below the portal. The Dragon snorted and tugged on the chain.

Nothing happened.

The Dragon tugged again.

While the shower of coins didn't occur, there were at least signs of movement from the portal.

"Did you know there was a manual over-ride for this thing?" Mister Lewis stuck his head through the portal.

The Dragon snarled and tugged on the chain a third time.

"That's not going to work," said Mister Lewis.

"Then I guess I'll be having a barbecue tonight, after all," bellowed The Dragon, swatting The Hippie out of the way and getting positioned directly underneath the portal.

The Dragon's head snapped back and Mister Lewis was barely able to get out of the way before flame shot straight up the portal. An instant later, the coins began to fall, but this time it was closer to a traditional shower. The Dragon's fiery breath was melting the coins as they fell. Some of the molten rhodium splashed on top of the coins lining the floor, but most of it went right down The Dragon's throat.

As the flames flicked out, The Dragon started coughing. The coins, no longer being melted, kept falling and another batch went into the throat and mouth before it closed.

The coughing turned to wheezing, then to choking as The Dragon's neck flailed wildly. The coins kept falling as The Dragon staggered and fell. The coins didn't stop falling until The Dragon was buried under a pile of rhodium that led almost to the ceiling.

Mister Lewis climbed down the pile and found The Hippie huddling in the corner, bruised from ricocheting coins and burned from the splatter of the liquid metal.

"What the hell is happening around here?" rasped The Hippie,

"You figure if The Dragon was casting coins," replied Mister Lewis. "That means the temperature of the fiery breath is lower than the vaporization point for rhodium. That kind of metal, it's a pretty high vaporization point, so it's not a great shock."

"And that's why I'm burned? Is... it dead?"

"It should be. You know how some musicians practice circular breathing when they play? Dragons aren't like that. All the air gets blown out when they breathe their fire. No more fire, the metal returns to its solid state and that's a very expensive blockage molded to the airways. If your friend isn't dead now, death isn't far off. And there'd be movement. Just be glad you got knocked out of the way and 'ole moneybags got right under the showerhead. I wasn't sure if it was going to play out like that."

"That seems..." The Hippie frowned and groped for phrase. "Reckless."

"That means so much, coming from you. Hey, you were going to die anyway if I didn't interrupt the shower. Just be glad something finally worked out for you this week."

"That reminds me," The Hippie sat up straight. "How am I supposed to get my money back if that thing is dead?"

Mister Lewis winced.

"Tell you what," he said slowly, as though giving instructions to a child. "Why don't you gather up some of those coins?

"But the crypto coins were supposed to be backed by gold, not rhodium?"

"Then it's your lucky day," Mister Lewis growled. "Rhodium's more expensive than gold. A lot more expensive. Get your refund, but do it fast. I want you out that door back there in 2 minutes."

"What happens in two minutes?"

"I get you out of here and figure out how to clean up this mess."

As The Hippie started filling pockets with coins, Mister Lewis stared at the pile in the center of the room. Part of a talon was only half-buried and still visible.

"I really should charge extra to disappear something that large," he muttered to himself.

Then he wondered where all those missing crates went to.